LOVE FOR THE HOLIDAYS

RAINBOW CENTRAL

ARIZONA TAPE

BLURB

With the approaching holidays and Ivy's ever-nosy family about her love life, a misunderstanding about her new roommate, Frances, gives her the perfect idea to avoid the yearly disappointment from her parents. A fake girlfriend. The rules are clear, it's just for the holidays.

-

Love For The Holidays is a sapphic fake-relationship contemporary romance set in the Rainbow Central series. This book will contain some recurring characters from other stories but no prior knowledge is needed to enjoy this holiday romance.

ONE

Ivy

Finding a housemate was tricky business.

I took a nervous sip from my hot cocoa, wishing I'd ordered something stronger to get me through this. The slender guy sitting on the other side of the table smiled in a seemingly reassuring way but it just upped the creep factor.

"So, the bathroom is shared, right?" he asked.

I nodded. "Yes, is that a problem?"

He smiled again. "No, no, not at all."

His eagerness put me off immediately and I mentally scratched his name off my list of potential roommates. While there was a good chance he was just trying to be amenable, I didn't like the vibes I was getting from him. If this was a job interview or something more serious, I'd fight harder to give him a fair chance, but considering I had to live with him... No thanks.

I folded my hands together, hoping to signal that the conversation was over. "Thank you for meeting me. I've got some other candidates so I'll be in touch."

"Umm... Okay?" He seemed confused that I wasn't making a decision on the spot. "Is it because I don't currently have a job? That's not going to be a problem for much longer, I'm pretty much guaranteed to start work on Monday."

"No, that's not a problem."

Relief cleared up his face. "So I got it?"

"No, I will let you know once I've met with everyone," I answered in as calm a tone as I could manage while glancing around for a server or someone that could help me in case this escalated. While the cosy bar wasn't super busy, it wasn't a super intimate place, which is why I'd chosen it for the first round of roommate meetings.

Luckily, I spotted my best friend at the glass entrance and some of the tension ebbed away. "Sorry, the next person is here so... Thanks."

"Right. I'll wait for your call," he said, checking out my best friend as she made her way to the table.

Oblivious to his stare, she unwound her long, green scarf and draped it over the back of the wooden chair. "Oof, it's chilly out there. What are you drinking?"

"Thank you for coming to this interview," I answered, a little louder than necessary. Just in case he was still listening.

Jenna seemed confused. "What? *Ivy*... Are you already drinking?"

"Please sit down, it's lovely to meet you." I waited until the guy left the café before I broke character. "Sorry, I told the last guy that you were the next candidate to get rid of him."

My best friend grimaced as she flagged a waitress. "Ouch, that bad?"

"No, he was perfectly polite. He just gave me weird vibes. If he was hitting on me on a night out, I'd be skipping him too."

"You can't choose a housemate based on who you're attracted to. That's guaranteed to end in disaster." She smiled at the approaching server, standing up to exchange cheek kisses. "Nini! Hey, girl, hey."

"What's up, Jenna? How are you? Coming to the

party later?" the waitress responded as she tossed her long hair over her shoulder.

"You know I love a good party. Where's the predrink?"

"At mine. We're starting at seven. There'll be some beer but you should bring your own booze. "Nini pulled out a little notepad from her apron and held it out. "What can I get you?"

Jenna gestured to my half-empty cup of cocoa. "What do you think? Want to get some drinks or something?

"God knows I could use something stronger after all the interviews. Seven candidates and I didn't like any of them. I'm never going to find a roommate at this point," I lamented. "What are you in the mood for? Cocktails?"

"Oh, so that's what you were doing," Nini commented. "I wondered if you were doing some kind of speed date type of situation on your own."

I almost choked on my drink. "No, no, no. No, it's not like that."

"Hey, I'm not judging. Pretty girls should date as much as they want," she responded, throwing in a wink for good measure.

My best friend chuckled. "Nice try, Nin, but you're out of luck. Ivy is straight."

"Is that so?" The waitress sighed dramatically. "What a shame. Oh well. Cocktails?"

"I'm game if you're game. I don't have class tomorrow," Jenna said. "The house cocktail is really good."

I nodded. "Let's do it. Maybe if I drink enough, I'll figure out a way I can make rent without having to get a housemate."

While the waitress went off to get our order, Jenna and I moved from the stiff table to one of the more comfortable booths in the corner of the bar. The faux-red leather and exposed lamps gave the whole place a bit of an old-school vibe that mashed well with the wooden ceiling. While we were settling in, a handful of women in the booth next to us recognised my best friend and greeted her like they hadn't seen her in years. Sometimes watching the warmth of which their community interacted made me feel a little left out. Not by anything Jenna was doing, she always did everything she could to include me, but still. It felt like there was a world out there that I wasn't a part of, that I could never understand. It was probably not fair to wish for those things when I enjoyed the privilege of being straight but every now and then, I envied my best friend for being able to connect so deeply with others like her. Even in very fleeting flings and affairs, the passion and intensity put my handful of relationships to shame. Guys just weren't like this, or at least, the guys I dated weren't like this.

Nini brought the drinks over and as she made her way back to the bar, one of the women in the other booth whistled as they watched her walk away.

"Is that okay?" I asked Jenna. "I thought we didn't like being catcalled."

My best friend chuckled. "That's her girlfriend."

"Oh, that makes more sense." I watched the server turn around once she reached the bar and threw a kiss back to her girlfriend. Except the entire group of girls reacted like it was aimed at them and with lots of gigging, the kiss was received.

I didn't really understand what that was about but if I asked Jenna about every weird thing her friends did, we'd be here for days.

I reached for the half-frozen cocktail and held it up for a toast. "Cheers."

"Cheers," Jenna answered, clinking her glass against mine. "I hope you like it."

The sweet, cherry flavour burst in my mouth and I moaned. "That's so good. I love that. Mmmm."

"Good, huh?"

"Really good. So what party are you going to later?"

"Oh, just an evening out with the lesbians. Pre-drinks at Nini's, then dancing here at Rainbow Central."

"Here?" I gestured around the cosy bar. "But it's a café, bar, pub situation."

"At night, they put the tables away and there's a DJ booth over there. Have I never taken you along?"

I shook my head. "No, I've only been here a couple of times, but it was during the day. We usually go to… The Royal?"

"Ah, it's not the same." Jenna sipped from her cocktail, the metal straw clicking against her teeth. "If you want, you can come along tonight."

"I can't, I've got work tomorrow." I sighed. "I got to admit, I do miss the freedom of being a student."

"Then why don't you just sign up again? The new school year has only just started. I bet you could enrol before the holidays come around. Or you could wait for the second semester?" Jenna suggested.

"No, I don't miss it *that* much. Dropping out was the best decision I ever made." I trailed my fingers up the narrow glass, drawing lines in the condensation. While I enjoyed partying, I didn't crave it nearly as much as when I was still a student. If anything, I preferred a casual drink like this over the craziness of a night out.

While I enjoyed my cocktail, some of the

conversation of Jenna's friends in the other booth made it over to our table.

"Are you serious?" The short-haired girl released a frustrated noise. "Thanks for nothing, Kim."

With a curious look on her face, Jenna turned around. "Everything okay, Frances?"

Frances tossed her phone on the table. "Yeah, fine. I like living under bridges."

Another girl in their group chuckled dryly. "That's a little dramatic."

"Kim promised that I could move into the spare room but apparently, she and Raquel couldn't agree over who got to keep the flat so they're *both* staying," the short-haired girl explained.

"Who wants to bet they'll be back together before the month is over?" Nini's girlfriend added.

The group of women all hummed in agreement. It was a shame I didn't know the people they were talking about but it sounded like drama.

"Hey, Ivy is looking for a housemate," Jenna quipped as she gestured to me, drawing the attention to our table. "It's a great place, only ten minutes from here, and I can personally guarantee that she's a fantastic roommate."

"I wish I could say the same about you but you're the one that's moving in with your girlfriend and leaving me in the lurch," I responded, giving her a bit of a playful nudge so she knew I wasn't actually upset. I was a little frustrated but not enough to deny my friend a shot at love.

The girl with the short hair, Frances, perked up. "You are?"

"She is. Hey, why don't you do your housemate interview thingy?" Jenna suggested. "You've got all your questions and info with you, right?"

She did make a good point. It felt a bit weird to interview a random stranger to live with me but that was exactly what I'd been doing beforehand. If anything, Frances was less of a stranger since she knew my best friend.

I shrugged as I handed her the printed page of my listing. Besides a couple of pictures of the flat, it also had the price and some other boring details. "Sure, why not? If you're interested?"

The other girl hopped out of the booth, surprisingly tall. She studied the page for a moment or two and smiled. "I'm interested."

TWO

Ivy

WHILE MY BEST friend helpfully swapped booths to make place for Frances, I dug my list with questions out from my bag. I hadn't expected to do another interview but I really wanted to find a housemate before the next month began. While Jenna was paying rent until I found someone new, I didn't want to make her pay for two places if it could be avoided.

A little nervous, I examined the tall girl in front of me. She was slender but muscular and pulling off her tank top in a way that I never could. I couldn't remember if Jenna ever mentioned her before but I suspected not. While Frances was a very beautiful girl, she wasn't my best friend's type. Maybe it was rude to be happy about that but the last thing I needed was for Jenna to fall for her and move back in when her moving out was the cause of all this mess. Or worse, have Frances move out so they could live together, leaving me without a housemate once again.

She folded her hands together and cocked her head to the side. "So what kind of questions do you want to ask me?"

Her question snapped me out of my thoughts and I pulled my attention to my list. "Right... Umm... Okay, I guess whether you're a student or working or... unemployed?"

"Student. I'm doing my last year in marine biology."

"Really?" Impressed, I jotted her answer down on my blank sheet. "Marine biology? That's interesting."

"I've always loved coral reefs. I'm doing my dissertation on the long-term effects of climate change and the greenhouse effect." She released an awkward chuckle. "But you probably don't need to know that."

I tried to smile reassuringly. "No, no, it's nice that you're passionate about your studies."

"I am." She held my gaze for a moment longer. "So are you a student too?"

Her question took me a little aback before I realised that it was perfectly normal that this interview was going both ways. Unlike the people that applied online and read some of my bio, Frances knew as little about me as I about her.

"I work part-time at a print shop while I figure out what I want to do with my life," I answered honestly. It wasn't the most glamorous job in the world but I liked the hours and the pay was decent.

"Aha, I see. Alright, what are your other questions?" she asked, capturing me in an intense but non-threatening gaze. Mostly, it just felt like she was making a real effort to pay attention.

"Umm, my other questions are a little unconventional, perhaps. On average, how often do you shower a week? What do you consider going to bed late and waking up early? Do you drink or smoke? Do you get angry easily and how often do you want to have friends over?"

Frances released a crystal laugh, her eyes lighting up with amusement. "This is more personal than a first date but alright. I shower every two days, more if I go running. I'm a bit of a night owl so I go to bed after midnight. I don't like waking up early. I drink occasionally, I don't smoke. Umm... What were your other questions?"

"Do you get angry easily and do you have your friends over a lot?" I added, trying to process her rapid stream of answers.

"Ah. I don't think I get angry easily unless I'm hungry, then I can be a bit of a grump. And… I guess I like having friends over but mostly, we hang out here, so." She finished her drink and pushed the empty glass to the edge of the table, where it was easy for the server to pick it up. "Is it my turn to ask questions now?"

I put my pen down, accepting the futility of writing down all her answers. "Sure."

A bright smile stretched across Frances' face. "How long do you take to get ready in the morning? Can I bring in furniture for the shared living spaces? How thin are the walls and if you lived with Jenna, I'm pretty sure I know the answer, but still, are you okay with me being a lesbian?"

"Good questions," I complimented, surprised that she came up with those on the fly.

She beamed. "Thank you."

"Okay, let's see. I'm not super fussy in the morning so maybe like… half an hour? The flat is fully furnished, except for the spare room, so it depends on what you want to bring. The walls are… not great. I used to put my headphones on when Jenna's girlfriend came over, if that's what you're asking. And I'm totally okay with the lesbian thing." I leaned back against the padded booth, hoping I answered everything well. "Anything else you want to know?"

"No, you seem like a cool chick. I can't make any decisions until I've seen the place though."

Fair. The only reason I didn't conduct interviews at home was so I could decide who I showed the house to. Maybe it was because the earlier candidates were so bad, but Frances seemed a pretty solid choice.

In a bit of an impulsive moment, I pulled my smartphone from my small handbag and unlocked it with my thumb. I pushed it across the wooden table. "Why don't you give me your number and we can arrange a viewing?"

"Sure." Frances reached for my phone and chuckled at my case with sunflowers. "Nice case."

"Thanks. I love sunflowers, they're my favourite."

"Adorable." She handed me my phone back and our fingers briefly touched. "Here's my number, Message me. I'm free pretty much whenever."

"Awesome, will do."

Frances rose from the booth to make her way back to her friends. As she turned around, something changed her mind and she faced me again, her arm stretched out. "It was nice to meet you, Ivy."

I quickly got up to take her hand, surprised by the firm but gentle shake. "Nice to meet you too."

THREE

Frances

I CHECKED the address on my phone against the number hanging next to the black front door. The little dead pot plant under the window and the row of doorbells confirmed that it was largely a student residence.

Confident that I found the place, I messaged Ivy that I was here. While I waited for her to let me in, I took a good look at the street. I liked the location, it was only a short bike ride to my campus and my favourite bar, Rainbow Central, was only a ten-minute walk away. Fifteen, when drunk.

The door shrieked open and revealed a much

more casually-clothed Ivy. She shot me a pretty radiant smile as she invited me in. "Hey, you made it."

"I did. Nice shirt," I commented, gesturing to the colourful flowers on her blouse. If I remembered correctly, there'd been flowers on her dress when we met too.

"Thank you. Come on up."

She preceded me up the narrow, winding stairs and I briefly wondered how anyone could get furniture up here. As we continued on, I made a conscious effort not to stare up Ivy's ass either. Beyond being impolite, that was not a good way to start a housemate arrangement. From what I heard from Jenna, she was straight anyway so more reason not to check her out.

After two sets of stairs, Ivy opened the door to the loft and let me in. The flood of natural light instantly caught my attention as I stepped into the flat. The open plan living area was spacious with a weathered dark-leather couch arranged in front of a tv and a small kitchen to the side. The hardwood floors looked like they'd be pleasant to walk on with bare feet and I liked the large skylight at the front of the room.

"Wow, nice," I commented, slowly taking in all the features.

"So this is the living area," Ivy added, gesturing around. "Pretty self-explanatory. Jenna and I spent a lot of time in here but we're also best friends. The rooms are big enough if you're more of a private person." She waved me along to the right side of the flat, opening one of three doors. "Bathroom. Toilet, sink, shower, no bath."

I shrugged. "I don't like baths."

"Perfect. And then over here, the room." She brushed past me to open the second door and I caught a faint whiff of her perfume. Floral, no surprise there.

She stepped away so I could have a look. I stopped in the middle, taking in the room, not that there was much to take in. The eggshell white walls looked clean and there was ample space for a double bed, a desk, and maybe some shelving. The large window outlooking the street was the best feature, no doubt.

"I like it," I voiced, pleasantly surprised by the place. While I'd have preferred to move in with my friend, this was better than returning to my parents. And as much as I enjoyed living with my best friend and her girlfriend, I was starting to feel like I was intruding on their lives. "So rent is…"

"Three-hundred a month, that included utilities. The contract is until the beginning of August, but you can get out if you pay rent until we find someone to move in."

"That's not bad." With another look at the wooden beams, I nodded. "Yeah, not bad at all. You spoke of other candidates so are there other applicants or…"

"No. I mean, I interviewed other people but they were weird," Ivy responded. "One girl asked whether she could walk around naked and someone else wanted to know how I felt about him growing weed in a kitchen cabinet."

I chuckled. "So no nudism and no horticulture. Got it."

A smile curled around the other girl's lips. "You can grow other things, just of the legal sort."

"You don't have to worry about that, I don't have green thumbs."

"But you like coral?"

"Corals are animals," I corrected her gently.

She slapped her forehead and chuckled. "Right, of course. I knew that, I'm just nervous. Sorry."

"No, I get it. Finding a new housemate is stressy." I followed her back into the living room, already feeling surprisingly comfortable. "Sounds like I've got fierce competition."

Ivy laughed as she settled at the rectangular kitchen table. She gestured to the chair across before getting up again. "I should've offered you something to drink. Tea? Coffee?"

"Just some water," I answered as I pushed my legs under the checkered tablecloth.

"You sure? I've got some lemonade as well, I think."

"Water is fine."

"Healthy," she commented as she grabbed me a glass and filled it at the tap. "Are you generally a healthy person?"

"Hmm, not overtly. I jog every now and then... I often end up ordering pizza after though," I admitted.

"Ah, a girl after my own heart." Ivy handed me the water and sat down opposite me, fiddling with her own glass. "So... Is there anything else you'd like to know?"

"Can I bring my aquarium?"

"Umm. Sure. Why not."

"Great. That's all I want to know." I looked around the place and nodded. "Yeah. I could see myself living here."

"Yeah?"

"Yeah."

Ivy seemed a little unsure but not necessarily in a bad way. She flattened the tablecloth and smiled.

"Okay. Alright. I guess we're doing this then? When would you want to move in?"

"When can I move in?"

"Well, the room is empty so as soon as you want. It's the middle of the month so we'll just calculate rent based on the days left."

I nodded. The whole ordeal felt surprisingly anticlimactic and I wasn't sure why. I'd just found a place to live that was affordable and in a great location. I should be over the moon and celebrate, but I wasn't sure if that was the right mood for the moment.

With a little finger drum on the table, I hoped to break some of the awkward tension. "Great. Great, great, great. I guess you should send me the contract and we'll make things official and stuff? I'll have to ask some of my mates to help but I should be able to move in next week."

"Yeah, sounds good! Alright. Awesome."

With a smile, I got up from the table. First meetings and arrangements like this were always awkward but they better get more comfortable quickly. I wanted to feel at ease in my own home.

Funny. This was my new home.

No, I shouldn't get too attached. That happened with Kim's place and that didn't turn out well. I would only allow myself to imprint once the paperwork was signed.

Ivy escorted me to the door. "I'll send the contract your way. It's pretty standard but if there's anything unclear, let me know. You can sign digitally. Do you know how?"

"Yup, that's fine." I lingered at the entrance. "Oh, could you send me the dimensions of the room as well? I want to make sure everything I want to bring fits."

"Of course." Ivy ran a hand through her strawberry blonde hair. "I guess I'll see you soon then."

I chuckled. "You will. See you soon."

FOUR

Ivy

A COUPLE OF DAYS LATER, Frances turned the whole flat upside down to move in her things. She wasn't bringing an excessive amount of furniture, the landing was just small and the shape of the flat made things awkward.

"Keep going, Tash!" one of her friends shouted as the two of them carried in a small armchair. "Pivot!"

"Right behind," someone else warned. "Careful, careful. You're going to smoosh me into the wall."

I had offered to help but Frances brought so many friends, there wasn't much to do for me. It wasn't quite clear whether any of them were her girlfriend but I'd never seen this many people rock up to help someone move. Apparently, the promise of pizza and beer had done the trick.

I did wonder why none of them had class but they were all college students, they were probably just skipping it. I remembered doing that without giving it a second thought. Now that I was working, that was no longer an option. I looked forward to my days off and being squashed on my couch while a bunch of sweaty strangers brought in enough clothes to fill a store wasn't quite what I imagined. But this was all for a good cause. With a new roommate moved in, I could stop worrying about rent and it would be nice to have some company with my best friend gone.

It was a little strange to feel on the outside in my own home. While all of Frances' friends were polite and some of them looked familiar, they were all caught up in their own little world. Showing off who could pick up the heaviest boxes, voicing decorating opinions while throwing compliments and flirtations around in the same breath. Two of them seemed in a relationship but it was hard to tell with the amount of affection going around.

Even though it was a group of girls, it felt like a completely different world. One I wasn't a part of, no matter how much Jenna tried to include me.

It was loud for hours before Frances' friends went home and a comfortable quiet returned to the flat, save for the stumbling in Jenna— Frances' room.

I got up from the couch and weaved my way through all the new stuff.

The door was open so I rapped my knuckles against the frame. "Knock knock. Need any help?"

Frances looked up from the floor where she was building a dresser or desk or something. "Hi. Ummm. Depends. Are you any good at building furniture?"

I took that as an invitation to enter and sit down across from her and the various pieces of plywood and screws. "I'm not *not* good at it?"

"Great. Cause this is either the world's worst built desk or I'm just terrible at it. I know, we're supposed to be good at building furniture but I guess I'm just a useless lesbian."

I released a soft chuckle. "I didn't realise you magically got woodworking skills once you started liking girls. And if it helps, if you asked Jenna for a screwdriver, you'd get a cocktail."

Frances' button nose wrinkled when she laughed. "Now that's a good thing."

I felt pleased that I managed to make my new roommate smile. Life would be so much better if we became friends so I could relax a little. New people stressed me out but this seemed to be going well. Frances was friendly and approachable but reserved enough that she didn't feel like she was invading my space. A very tricky balance and I was grateful for it.

"Hand me the instructions," I said, determined to help her out. She handed me the stapled sheets and I studied the pictures, trying to put the images to the pieces on the floor. It didn't look overly complex but I wasn't going to tell Frances that. "Okay... We're supposed to start with pieces A and B, which are those big planks over there. They need to be put together with screws J. There should be four of them."

Frances held up two plastic bags with two types of screws in them. "Yes, but which ones are they?"

"Ummm... Left. No. Right. Wait, let me check the instructions again." I compared the images to the hardware but neither of them matched the picture. "Hang on, this doesn't make any sense. Are you sure you're not missing any pieces?"

Frances adjusted her position, folding her legs together. "Nope, the box is empty."

"Okay, okay... Oh, look. I think— Yes, I think these are the right ones cause we need two more J screws later so that's six."

"Ooh. That's clever," Frances complimented. She grabbed a screwdriver with a yellow handle and held it out to me. "Want to hold pieces or want to do the screwing?"

I chuckled. "I'm a little out of practice on the latter, I'll hold things."

My new roommate laughed. "Touché. Alright, I think this is the frame."

We worked together with surprising ease, putting up her desk without needing to resort to daytime drinking or spiralling into a fight. It probably helped that we didn't know each other well enough for that.

When we were done, Frances pushed the desk against the wall under her window and nodded. "I like it. Thanks for helping me out."

"No worries. Just shout if you need my help for anything else."

"I might leave the rest of the unpacking till tomorrow, I'm beat."

"I'll leave you to it." I got up from the floor and stretched the initial stiffness out of my muscles. "Woah, I'm getting old."

The other girl chuckled. "What are you talking about?"

"I'm almost twenty-one. Old. Being a working woman really takes a toll on the body," I joked.

Frances laughed even more. "You're hilarious. Twenty is so young. I remember twenty, good times."

"How old are you?"

"Twenty-two."

"Oh, so you're basically a grandma at this point," I teased, glad the banter was coming easily.

Frances pretended to hold a walking stick as she paced through the room. "My, my, where did I leave my dentures?"

"Brilliant impression. My grandma actually used to keep losing her spare teeth so whenever we visited, me and my brother always played a game to see who could find them first. In hindsight, a little disturbing." I took a step back, not wanting to impose. "Anyway, I'll let you rest. You must be exhausted."

"I am. Moving is the worst but I'm glad I don't have a lot of stuff," she said, pausing as she exited the room and got a view of the packed living room. "Well, *unloading* is done. I'll move these boxes first thing tomorrow. I'm a little hungry. Would you mind if I cooked? I've got this thing where you only live somewhere after you've cooked a meal in the place."

I smiled, gesturing to the fridge. "Knock yourself out. You're welcome to use whatever is in the fridge or there's a little store right around the corner if my old peppers won't do."

"I'm sure they'll do just fine." Frances ripped open

one of the boxes and pulled a large, weathered pan from it. She twirled it before putting it on the hob. "Do you like pasta? It's one of my favourite, quick go-to meals."

I nodded, my attention drawn to her toned arms. "I love pasta."

"Great. And you're sure it's okay if I use your vegetables?"

"Oh yeah. If you're making me food, you can have my car. Or a kidney cause I don't have a car," I answered, joining her in the kitchen area and taking up the one chair that was free. "I don't like cooking."

"I do." Frances flashed me a wide smile. "Sounds like we're a good match."

FIVE

Frances

WAKING up in a new place was always a bit weird but I didn't feel too stressed. With a satisfied sigh, I took in my new surroundings. The tilted ceiling gave my room a cosy nook for my bed and with my familiar sheets, it wasn't so different. Sunlight streamed in through the large roof window and the warm light made the wood glow. Besides the desk we put together yesterday, the room was bare but had a lot of potential. I had high hopes for the place. There was no reason why I couldn't be happy here.

I swung my legs out, curling my toes into the once-fluffy rug. From the noises on the other side of the door, I could tell my new roommate was already awake. I pulled a loose tank top over my head and some boxers to serve as shorts. Still yawning, I made my way into the living area, not surprised to find a barely-awake Ivy in pink pyjamas at the kitchen table with a steaming mug of coffee.

"Morning," she mumbled, waving sleepily.

"Hey." I pointed at the gurgling coffee machine on the counter. "Can I have some of that?"

"Help yourself."

"I might have to borrow a mug." I gestured to the stacks of boxes occupying most of the living space. "I'm not sure where mine are."

Ivy pointed at one of the cupboards, her eyes only half open.

"Thanks." I rummaged through the assortment of mugs, picking one with a funny crab with a party hat on it. "This is fun."

She slurped from her mug. "Jenna gave that to me when my ex gave me the crabs. He was such an asshole. Sorry, that was TMI."

Yikes. I slowly put the mug back and picked another one with floral print, hoping this didn't have a weird story attached to it. She didn't say anything so I filled it up with steaming hot coffee and sat down opposite of her.

We sat in silence, each drinking our beverage and

adjusting to the morning. It was a strangely intimate moment for two strangers, but it didn't feel weird. I was getting ready for class, she was probably on the way to work, this was just the first of many mornings we'd spent like this.

"You work in a printshop, right?" I said, not opposed to some small talk.

Ivy nodded. "Yup, it's not very glamorous but it pays the bills."

"So what's your dream job like?"

"Gah, now you're asking good questions. If I knew that, I wouldn't be working at the print shop," she replied, finishing her coffee. Her chair scraped over the tiles as she stood up and put her mug in the sink. "I'm toasting some waffles, you want some?"

Not quite my desired breakfast but I hadn't done any shopping yet and I didn't want to sound ungrateful. "Sure, thanks."

In silence, Ivy filled the two slots of the toaster with waffles and waited until they popped up. The nutty, slightly sweet smell filled the kitchen and after my first bite, I had to admit they were tastier than expected.

Ivy yawned as she cleared our plates away. "I've got to get dressed."

"Same. My conservation physio class starts at nine and our professor isn't very lenient on latecomers." I rotated my shoulder and wobbled my head back and forth. "I guess I'll see you in the evening?"

"Yup, I usually get back home around six-ish."

"Cool! I've got classes all day, so… Yeah. Umm, how did you and Jenna do dinner? Did you cook together or do your separate thing?" It felt oddly domestic to coordinate our schedules but it was good to figure out these practicalities and expectations.

Ivy paused to think. "Well, we each had a shelf in the fridge and a shared one. We usually made plans or texted each other if we didn't. But we don't have to do it that way. Jenna and I have been friends since we were eleven so…"

"And we've only just met. No worries, we can play things by ear," I assured her.

"Yeah, sounds good. Do you have my number?"

"Yup, I'll text you," I promised.

My roommate gave me a thumbs up before she disappeared into the bathroom. I heard the shower turn on and realised I should've asked how long she was going to be, considering I also had to get ready. Oh well, too late.

To bridge the time, I pushed some of my boxes into my room so I could unpack them later. After I worked up quite a sweat, I was relieved when I heard the bathroom door open. Not wanting to accidentally walk in on Ivy in just a towel, I waited until I was sure she was back in her room.

I rushed through my morning routine and by the time I was ready to leave, it looked like Ivy was already gone. It was a bit strange to be in the flat without her, but I'd have to get used to it. After all, this was my home now too.

SIX

Ivy

IT WAS strange to know that I wasn't going home to an empty flat. Even though Jenna had only moved out two weeks ago, it had felt a lot longer. Time moved slowly when I was on my own. But now, I had a new housemate. And while I didn't know Frances very well yet, I was excited to have a new friend.

I dug my house keys out of my bag and pushed into the flat, climbing the stairs. While I wasn't in bad shape, I was huffing and puffing by the time I got up to the landing. When I showed Frances up, I'd purposefully pretended like the two flights didn't bother me.

While I caught my breath, a savoury smell filled my nose. Surprisingly, it came from my flat. I unlocked the front door, stepping into the living room.

From by the stove, Frances turned around, spatula in hand, and waved. "Hey hey."

"Hi. Something smells good." I hung my coat up and made my way to the kitchen, trying my best not to drool.

"Just a boring pasta pesto, nothing fancy," she said, looking adorable in her apron. She tossed in a bunch of cherry tomatoes and whistled as she combined them with her cooked spaghetti. "There's enough for two, if you're hungry."

My stomach rumbled. "Are you sure that's okay? That's the second time you've cooked."

She smiled. "It's fine, I like cooking."

"Okay, if you're sure. But I'll pay you back. Or we can buy some groceries together or something," I decided, not wanting to take advantage of my new roommate. That would just end in tears.

Frances continued whistling a little tune as she finished her dish and I set the table, wanting to contribute in some way.

"Ready," the other woman announced as she put

the steaming pan on the cork potholder. A fragrant, herby smell rose with the steam as she filled up our bowls.

"So how was school?" I asked, taking my first bite. The fresh taste of basil and mozzarella cheese filled my mouth, the combination one of my favourites. "Yum, this is delicious."

"I'm glad you like it. And school was ehh. I like most of my classes but I'm glad this is my last year. How was work?"

I finished chewing. "Ehh too. We printed things, had jams, ran out of paper. Regular stuff."

Frances chuckled, her laugh bright and slightly hoarse. "You live an exciting life, Ivy."

"So exciting. Some clients act like it's life or death when a printer breaks."

I studied the woman across the table, not sure how I was supposed to feel. It wasn't fair to call her a stranger in my home because this was her home now too. But I didn't know her. Or barely. There was every chance that she was secretly a spy, or a serial killer, or a flat-Earther.

Frances paused mid-bite, having noticed my staring. "Like my face?"

I quickly averted my gaze. "Sorry, I was just thinking how it's weird we live together but don't know each other at all."

"Okay." She put her fork down. "What do you want to know?"

"I don't know." I fiddled with the tablecloth on my side.

"You know there are lists for this," Frances remarked, reaching for her phone. "They're usually for first dates but the premise stands."

"That's a fun idea. I suppose this is kind of like a platonic first date. What's first on the list?"

"Hmm, hmmm, hmm, let me see. Okay, there's a list with one-hundred questions. That's a bit overkill. Twenty-one questions to ask a guy. Not relevant. Ah, here we go. The only ten questions you'll ever need." Frances released a scoff. "That's confident."

"A little," I agreed. "What does it say?"

"Okay, first question. What makes you unique?" Frances read, her eyebrows furrowing together. "Wow, diving right in."

"With the worst question ever," I added. "I don't know what makes me unique. That's impossible to answer."

"Agreed. I'm skipping to the next one. What would you consider a perfect weekend?"

"Gosh… Hmmm… Okay, sleeping in, obviously."

She laughed. "Obviously."

"Then brunch with some nice tea. A light activity,

perhaps. I'd probably want to see Jenna and some of our other friends. But there would also be time to sit at home, read a good book, have a nice long bath. Oh, dinner at a local place, something cosy. No fancy restaurant or something. And then on Sunday… Gah, I don't know. The same?"

"Sounds good. For me… Party hard on Saturday, light hangover on Sunday that's gone by dinner so I can eat something greasy and trashy. Like fries or a nice kebab. I do love a good kebab."

"Ooh, I want to change my answer and add a good party to it too," I exclaimed. "But I'll skip the hangover on Sunday. Although I want a piece of that kebab. Heck, I want one for myself."

"A girl after my own heart." Frances checked her phone and smiled. "Oh, this is fun. Most embarrassing story. And the crabs don't count."

"It doesn't get much worse than that."

"It's super common though. Are you done eating?"

I pushed my empty plate towards her. "Yeah, it was super tasty. Thank you. I'll do the dishes, it's only fair."

"Awesome, I hate doing dishes."

"I don't mind it. It's the cooking bit that I don't like. Pretty sweet trade-off if you ask me," I answered, getting up to sort out the pots and pans. It wasn't until I was crowding Frances by the sink that I realised how impractical this was.

I tried to reach the sink but almost got tangled with my new roommate.

She tried to step aside at the same time as I did, which only added to the awkward dance. We moved at the same time again, stuck in the small space between the white counter and the kitchen table.

"Stop." Frances reached out, her hands finding my upper arms as she steadied me. She gently moved me to the side, breaking the stalemate. "There."

"That was so cliché," I remarked as I took place in front of the sink.

"So cliché," Frances agreed with a smile as she sat back down. "Want to do more questions or you done with our platonic date?"

I turned the tap on, enjoying the hot water on my hands. "No, I'm happy to do more questions."

"Okiedokie. Ah, here. What's your biggest pet peeve?"

"When someone borrows something and they never give it back. If you wanted to keep it, why not just buy it?" I blurt out.

"That's such a good point. I hate when people do that. Although my biggest pet peeve is people putting their phone on speaker in a public place. It's so rude!"

We talked and laughed so much, I was done with the dishes in no time. While they were drying, we moved to the couch and got settled in with a glass of wine. Talking to Frances was easy and effortless, not something I usually experienced when meeting new people.

A quick glance at my phone confirmed that we'd been chatting for hours already, but we still had plenty of things to discuss.

Frances propped her arm under her head, leaning on the back of the couch as she read another question. "What would you like to get better at? Oh, that's a good one."

I took a sip of wine to gain some time before I answered, more truthfully than I expected. "I wish I was better at being funny. I know, it's a little sad, but I'm just so bad at it."

"Funny how?"

"I don't know, like jokes? But just general funny. Jenna is hilarious, she can always make people feel at ease by making them smile and I just say awkward things. Like this morning, why did I tell you I've had crabs? That's not something you want to know. That's not something anyone wants to know. It's just embarrassing."

Frances smothered a chuckle. "I'm sorry but it's

kind of funny. But yeah, definitely not something you should bring up on an actual first date."

"Agreed. So is it your turn now to answer the same question?"

"I can. I wish I could be better at doing feminine things. I've got lots of girl friends and we hang and gossip and chat, but that's not how it always used to be." She paused for a bit, pushing her pasta back and forth on the plate. "I was always the odd one out as a child. I didn't fit in with the girls and their dresses and dolls, but I wasn't a boy either. They knew better than to tease me but... not fun."

I took my time finding a thoughtful response, not quite managing to come up with something. Instead, I reached out to touch Frances' hand. "I'm glad things got better."

"Yeah, they did. I found my community, my people. I've got loads of friends now and I'm happy with how I am. But even so, when I'm in public or more gender-defined spaces, I always feel a little self-conscious when I show up in a suit or something."

"Pah, please. Come on, I'm sure you rock any suit you wear!" I exclaimed, not having any trouble picturing Frances in a waistcoat and tie.

The other girl swatted the air. "Oh, you flatter me."

"No, I mean it. You shouldn't feel insecure, you're gorgeous." It wasn't until my compliment left my mouth that I wondered about the implications of it. I was so used to raising up my friends about their clothes or hair or general appearances, it came as second nature. But Frances was gay. Did compliments mean something else to the lesbians? I didn't know and it wasn't like Jenna was a good comparison. We'd known each other for years, there was no attraction or chemistry. We were like sisters.

But Frances…

Frances was new. And I didn't want to give her the wrong impression or lead her on.

I quickly downed the rest of my wine and yawned. "Woah, I'm tired. I think the alochol is really getting to me. I might need a little lie down."

"Right. Yeah, of course. Sorry, I didn't mean to keep you this long." Frances jolted up, looking quite apologetic.

"No, no. Don't be sorry. I was having loads of fun talking to you. You're really easy to talk to." Dang, another compliment. I really had to watch that. Or at least, I'd have to ask Jenna about it. "Well… Goodnight."

If Frances was confused or rattled, she didn't show it. "I had a great time getting to know you on our platonic date. Goodnight."

With a last smile, I made my way to my room. It wasn't time for bed yet, so I settled on my little one-seater with the intention of reading something. While I plugged in my reading device, I was hyper aware of Frances' presence on the other side of the door. It was strange to have a housemate again after a couple of weeks of having the place completely to myself. But not in an unpleasant way. I'd just have to get used to it.

SEVEN

Frances

My vibrating phone alerted me to the incoming call and I sighed when I saw who it was. Mum. Great. Why did she always call at the most inconvenient time?

"Hello," I answered curtly, trapping the device between my shoulder and ear so I could keep packing my bag.

"Fran! Daaaaaarling. How've you been?"

"Good, I'm getting ready for school. What's up?"

"Your father and I have *just* booked the most wonderful vacation. We're leaving in a couple of days for the Caribbean. We're doing two full weeks to see all the islands. We'll even get to interact with the locals!"

"Two weeks?"

"Yes, but don't worry, we'll be back for the holidays so we can celebrate as a family. We'll have to miss your birthday but your gift is on the way and we've put some extra money in your bank account. You should treat yourself to something nice."

I sighed. It wasn't like this was the first birthday they'd missed but it still stung. I would've argued if I thought it would make a difference, but it never did. Instead, I just pretended to sound chipper. "Thanks. Have a nice trip. Say hello to Dad."

"I will. Byeee!"

With a bitter taste in my mouth, I threw my phone on my bed. It hit my pillow and bounced on the floor with a loud bang. I didn't bother picking it up. Instead, I wrapped my arms around my legs and rested my chin on my knees. `

Why were they like this? She hadn't even asked if I found somewhere new to live. Their degree of caring only extended as far as asking if I had enough money. Like if they gave me enough, they weren't neglectful parents. I supposed lots of people didn't even have the money, but it always made me feel cheap when they thought an expensive present would make up for their absence.

A soft knock sounded as my door was cracked open. "Hello? You okay? I heard a loud noise."

"Yeah, everything's fine. Come in," I called back.

Ivy shuffled into my room, a worried look on her face. "What are you doing on the floor?"

"Huh? Oh, I was packing my bag." I gestured to the box with my course material. Once I put my shelf up, I'd be able to put those away but I'd prioritised building other things. Like my bed, the table for my tank, and the dresser for my clothes.

My new roommate lingered at the entrance. "You sure you're okay? I know I don't know you very well but you seem down."

"Yeah, it's fine. Just my stupid parents." I gathered a breath as I got up and mustered a smile. "You're not at work?"

"Nope, I don't work today. Ooh, what's this?" She eyed up the new tank next to the door and virtually pressed her nose against the glass. "Where are your fishies? Your aquarium is empty."

I grinned. "I don't have any. Just coral."

"Huh. Never seen a tank like that before. Do they have names?"

"They don't."

"That's sad. Pets should have names."

A wave of affection washed over me at her calling my coral pets. Not a lot of people considered them worthy of much attention but they'd always fascinated me.

She gestured to a pink perky specimen. "I like this one. It's cute. It kind of looks like a curly mushroom."

I chuckled. "You're not far off. That's a weeping willow, it belongs to the Toadstool group. It's one of the first types I got, they're great for beginners." I joined her by the tank, pointing to a tree-like type that moved with the water. "But this is my favourite. It's a sinularia. They come in all kinds of colours, but yellow is my favourite."

"It looks like it has tiny hands."

"It does, doesn't it?" I smiled, feeling a lot lighter than before. I loved talking about coral and Ivy's inquisitiveness really made me feel like she was interested.

I caught her eye and her lips tugged up in a smile. "Your coral are pretty cute."

"You're pretty cute," I blurted out before I fully processed what I was saying. "Sorry, that was uncalled for."

To my relief, Ivy didn't seem deterred or offended in the slightest. She just chuckled. "No worries. I've been around Jenna's friends, you lesbians are a flirty bunch. I just take it as a compliment. Except that one girl who said she'd like me to ride her dildo. I didn't appreciate that."

I groaned. "That's so bad. I wouldn't like that either."

"Yeah, I wasn't too sad when she moved to another city."

"I'll try better to reign in the flirty," I promised her.

"It's not your fault I'm so irresistible," Ivy joked as she dramatically gestured to herself. "Hey, what are you doing today?"

I glanced at my bag. "I was going to go to class but I'm not really in the mood. You have anything in mind?"

"Well, I was going into the city centre to buy some things for the flat. We need toilet cleaner and we're out of vacuum bags. Want to tag along? I mean, we could grab some coffee in a nice café, maybe eat something, look at clothes. You don't have to come for just errands," she quickly added.

"Toilet cleaner and vacuum bags? Sounds awful," I responded in a light, cheery tone. I was surprised that Ivy was laughing at my backwards sense of humour so I kept going. "Shopping is my personal nightmare. Let's do it!"

Ivy snorted. "Hey, if you don't want to come, you don't have to."

I ushered her out of my room, following closely. "No, it sounds fun when you say it. Shall we pick up some window cleaner as well?"

She gave me a gentle push. "Hey! Don't be upset with me for adulting. The flat doesn't clean itself."

"I wish. I hate cleaning."

We chatted all the way to the city, the conversation light and easy. Even running errands was fun with Ivy's chipper attitude. After buying all the necessary cleaning stuff, we made our way back to the tram stop.

"Ah, can you smell that?" Ivy inhaled deeply, wafting the air in her face. "That's the smell of fresh waffles. Oh, I love it. I want some. Oh I *want* some but I can't."

I frowned. "Why not?"

"I'm trying to lose weight." Ivy patted her stomach. "I've put on a few."

With a raised eyebrow, I did a double take of my housemate. Her flowery dress was flowy but fitted nicely around her waist. She was a little heavier in the chest area but nothing to complain about. Nothing… at… all.

"Well?" We stopped in front of a window with badly decorated mannequins and Ivy gestured up and down herself. "Do you think I'm fat?"

"No. No, you've got a great figure," I remarked,

checking out both our reflections. "I mean, compared to me, I'm just a plank or a ruler."

"Don't say such mean things. You're so tall and you've got those wonderful cheekbones. I'm just a puffy racoon."

I smothered a chuckle. "Racoon?"

"Yeah, because of the bags under my eyes."

"You're funny. My best friend's girlfriend loves racoons. She calls them trash bandits. They actually went on a first date to a petting zoo to see racoons."

Ivy chortled as we continued on. "I didn't realise that was a thing."

"Apparently." I took a deep breath and sighed. "Those waffles do smell amazing. Let's get some. Stop worrying about your weight, you're gorgeous and you deserve a waffle."

"You know what, I do deserve a waffle. I went running like... two weeks ago. And I had a salad for lunch yesterday. Arguably, there was bacon on it and cheese, lots of cheese, but there were looooots of vegetables," Ivy rambled, sounding like she was trying to convince herself.

I gently nudge her in the direction of the cart. A man with hair the same colour as his golden-brown waffles danced back and forth behind the waffle irons, filling them up with fresh batter. He opened up one of the machines and a gust of steam rose up, the smell filling the air. I could tell people were turning their heads and joining the queue to get their hands on one.

It only took a couple of minutes before it was our turn. I dug out my wallet for some cash and handed it to the vendor. "Two waffles. Right, Ivy, you're having a waffle?"

She nodded. "Yes, please."

"Yeah, two waffles," I confirmed.

The vendor reached over his little display and handed us a fresh, hot sugar waffle in a napkin. "There you go."

Ready to devour my waffle, we picked a spot on a nearby bench and dug in. For a moment, everything disappeared but the warm, gooey sugar and delicious waffle. It was heaven in a napkin and I wanted to eat a thousand of them.

"This is amazing," I mumbled with my mouth full. "Oh my god, this is good."

Ivy sighed dreamily as she savoured every bite. "So good!"

I ate the whole thing in record time and licked my fingers for good measure. As soon as the last bite was gone, I eyed up the vendor and the rest of his waffles. Maybe I could have another...

"Hey, Frances!" A voice called from the left.

I turned towards the noise and spotted one of my

friends with a lot of shopping bags. "Hey hey! Linda, how are you? Wow, did you buy out a shop?"

She laughed. "I tried but my credit card didn't let me. Who is this? A new girlfriend?"

"No, no, this is my new housemate. Ivy, Linda, Linda, Ivy," I introduced, quickly clearing up any misunderstandings or notions about who Ivy was to me. I didn't want her thinking I'd been telling people she was something she wasn't.

"Oooh, right." Linda snapped her fingers. "Yeah, sorry I couldn't help you move. I wasn't in town but I'll definitely come to the housewarming party. When is that?"

That was a good question. I glanced at Ivy, trying to read her expression. I wanted to check with her first before inviting all my wild friends over but I didn't want to put her on the spot. "I'm not sure yet but I'll let you know."

Linda snapped her fingers rhythmically, swaying back and forth. "Great. I love a good party, you know I love a good party. I got to go, I'm meeting Crescent. See you soon."

I waved as she pushed through the crowd, making every get out of her way with the sheer space all her bags took up. I waited until she was out of earshot before turning to Ivy. "Would it be okay to throw a housewarming? I know my friends can be a bit crazy but they're really fun. We'd just do pre-drinks and then go dancing somewhere."

Ivy smiled. "Of course, it's your house."

"Yeah, but we live there together and I want to check these things with you."

"You're already more considerate than Jenna ever was." She leaned against the back of the bench, enjoying the breeze playing with her strawberry blonde ponytail. "I know it's early days but I'm glad we overheard your call in Rainbow Central. You're a nice housemate."

"Thanks." I gave her a playful nudge. "You're not so bad yourself."

EIGHT

Frances

I SMILED to myself as I changed the tv, happy to have the flat to myself for the moment.

It was just before the housewarming party would start so I was making the most of the last minutes of alone time. Girls' night out could get pretty crazy.

While flicking through shows, I heard stumbling on the landing and the jingling of keys in the lock. I was still getting used to identifying all the new sounds but that one was pretty easy.

I turned to say hello to Ivy but instead, I was looking at a life-size cardboard cut-out of a bear with a Christmas hat.

"What the fuck is that?" I exclaimed.

Ivy's head appeared from behind the bear. "Hiya! Sorry, did I scare you?"

"No, just… I'm surprised. Why do you have a bear cut-out?"

My roommate wrestled with the cardboard as she tried to find a place for it in the flat. "Someone ordered it but cancelled after we already printed it. My boss asked if I wanted it and I didn't know how to say no. So… say hello to our new roommate."

"Why didn't you just put it in the trash?"

"I wanted to but it just felt wrong to hurt the bear and my boss seemed so happy that I wanted it." She gave it a gentle pat. "He's cute, isn't he?"

I released a full belly-laugh. "He's incredibly large."

"But he's got a Christmas hat. He's festive!"

"That's true. Maybe we can put him by the front door so if a burglar tries to break in, they'll get the shock of their life."

Ivy cocked her head to the side as she undid her jacket. "But why would a burglar try to rob us on the second floor?"

"That's a good point," I conceded.

"I'll put him over here for now," my roommate said, pushing the bear against the wall. "Looks good. What time does the party start again?"

I checked my phone. "Tash said she'd be here fifteen minutes ago so… half an hour?"

"Great. Then I've got time to jump in the shower and wash off all the ink. You have no idea about all the places I've got ink."

Her statement conjured an interesting image but I quickly shook that out of my head. Roommate. Straight. There were enough reasons why I shouldn't even entertain these thoughts.

While Ivy showered and got ready in her room, I picked a show to distract myself, grateful when my best friend texted that she was downstairs. Eager to get the party started, I buzzed her in and waited for her on the landing.

She arrived with a bottle of wine and a large smile. "Fraaaaaan! Ooh, I'm so excited to see everything furnished."

"Come in, come in." I gave her a quick hug before I ushered her into the flat. Of course, she'd seen the main areas when she helped me move in.

It didn't take long for some of my other friends to arrive with more booze and good moods. I gathered them around the table and quickly, a jubilant and joyful atmosphere filled the flat. I never realised how many friends I had until I had to find chairs for them all.

Like any good party, corks were pulled and caps

popped as soon as possible. Everyone was in the mood to drink and chatter quickly took over the kitchen. I glanced at Ivy, hoping she wasn't feeling too overwhelmed with all my friends. I insisted that she joined my housewarming so she didn't feel left out, but now I worried that I'd put her in an awkward situation.

Luckily, it didn't seem so. She was happily chatting with Tasha, which reassured me a little. I didn't want to start our roommate situation with bad blood. This was a good place and I wanted to live here for a while.

"Who wants to play drinking games?" Berry shouted, earning cheers from everyone.

That settled it then. Games were always fun and it would be easy for Ivy to join in.

"What are we playing?" I questioned, pulling my chair closer to the kitchen table and squeezing in between my best friend and my roommate.

"Ring of fire," Berry answered in that matter-of-factly tone that always got her what she wanted.

From the lack of protest, it seemed everyone agreed. I directed my attention to Ivy. "Do you have a pack of cards?"

"Yeah, I must do. Let me find it." She got up from her chair, slightly unsteady on her feet. She squeezed past me, her hand trailing along my shoulder. I watched her sway to her room, bemused by how tipsy she already was. We'd barely started drinking and she was already hazy. She must be one of those lightweight types.

It didn't take very long for her to return with a pack of cards, held up like a sacred relic. "I got the cards!"

More cheers broke out and she was welcomed warmly by all my friends. From the sounds of it, some of them vaguely knew her as Jenna's friend. That would probably change now that I lived here. At least it was reassuring to know that Ivy really didn't have a problem with my sexuality.

She sat back down next to me and handed the cards to Berry who fanned them out face-down in a circle. "Ring of fire is very simple. Every card has a rule. If you don't know the rules yet, you'll learn. Alright, Frances, you're up first!"

I took a sip from my beer. "Why me?"

"It's your party!"

That was a good point. I reached out and since it didn't matter which card I picked, I just took the one closest to me. "Two of hearts! That's two for you. I pick... Berry! That's for making us play this game."

Everyone laughed as Berry graciously took two sips of her glass of wine. "Alright, alright. We're going clockwise so Tash, you're up."

One by one, everyone picked their card and inflicted the rule on the group. As the game progressed, more and more booze was consumed. The chatter and conversation got louder while everything became funnier. While I wasn't immune to the effect of alcohol, I didn't get drunk nearly as quickly as some of my friends. It was amusing to see everyone lose their inhibitions and go crazy.

Once it was my turn, I picked another random card. "Oh, eight of spades!"

"Pick a date, pick a date," the girls chanted.

I pointed my card at Ivy. "You can be my date."

A slight blush tinted her cheeks, but that could've been the alcohol. She accepted the card, her fingers brushing against mine. "What does that mean?"

"Whenever I have to drink, you have to drink," I explained, quickly pulling my hand back.

She snickered cutely. "Fun!"

"My turn," Tash exclaimed, pulling her own card. "Ooh, another eight. I pick Frances as my date."

Everyone howled, except for Ivy. She looked at her eight, then at mine, the calculations coming a little slower than usual. "Wait, if Tasha has to drink, then Frances has to drink... Then I have to drink?"

Berry clapped her hands, barely able to speak from laughter. "Yes! Isn't this game genius? It's a chain of dates!"

My roommate groaned. "Oh, I don't know if my liver is going to survive this. It's a good thing I don't have to work tomorrow."

It was a good thing, indeed. The game kept going round and round, with more cards being pulled, and more bottles being opened. Almost all sips were awarded to Tash, which triggered the chain, making me drink, making Ivy drink. Everyone, especially Berry, was taking great pleasure in the results of the game until Ivy picked an eight of her own and assigned it to her.

I almost choked with laughter from seeing Berry's sour face and I felt proud of my roommate for giving my friend a taste of her own medicine. She always won at games so it was great to see her dragged down with us.

As the evening went on, and everyone got drunker, the card game was abandoned in favour of just drinking and chatting.

"I love wine," Ivy announced drunkenly, her cheeks flushed. The drink in her glass was sloshing back and forth, her grip unstead. "Wine is so magical."

I laughed. "You're so drunk. How much have you had?"

"Not a lot," she hiccuped. "I used to be able to

drink much more, y'know? But ever since I started working, my tolerance just went splooosh."

A wave of affection rolled over me and I gave her an amicable nudge. "You're alright, you know that? I'm glad that you picked me to be your roommate."

"Ditto. Oh, I think I need the bathroom." She got up, unsteady on her feet. On her way, she said something to Tash who bursted out in laughter and gave her a high five. If anyone was looking from the outside in, they'd never know Ivy was the odd one out. Everyone seemed to get along with her and it didn't escape my notice how Linda and Crescent were making eyes at her either.

I joined them on the couch, a cold beer in hand. "Don't even think about it."

Linda shot me an innocent look. "Think about what?"

"Ivy is straight."

A confident smirk graced Crescent's lips. "That doesn't stop me. Or them."

"Fine, but don't tell me I didn't warn you when the straight girl breaks your heart," I said.

"Oooh, you like her," Linda exclaimed, sounding surprisingly clear despite her swimming eyes. "You've got a crush on your roommate?"

"What? No! No, I don't have a crush on Ivy. I'm just telling you so you don't chase after her all night."

"Are you sure she's straight?" Crescent grunted as she pushed herself up from the dingy couch so she could get a better look at my housemate. "I think I've seen her before. Didn't she make out with Cassie?"

"No, no, that was Lottie," Linda corrected her. "She used to be straight but they had a brief fling. I heard she got married to a man not so long ago though. Cassie was pretty upset about it."

"Oooh, right. Lottie. Yeah. This is why you don't date straight women," Crescent said. It took a moment for her to realise the irony of her words and tear her gaze away from Ivy. "Yeah, I think I'll pass on Ivy after all."

"Good idea," I responded, earning a sly grin from Linda. "Don't look at me like that. I don't have a crush on Ivy! Jeesh, she's my roommate. I'm not stupid enough to do my roommate."

Before they could make all kinds of comments, I got up and raised my hands to get everyone's attention. "Shall we move this party to Rainbow Central?"

The excited response told me everyone was raring to go and it took a surprisingly short time to gather everyone's stuff. Everyone was singing and getting ready in the mood when Ivy returned from the bathroom, looking just slightly more steady.

"Hey, we're going dancing. You coming?" I proposed.

She yawned. "No, thanks. I don't think I have more left in me."

"Aw, come on. It'll be lots of fun. First round is on me, eight-date." I grabbed her hand, pulling her along.

"Nooo, don't tell me the game continues," she complained, although she didn't sound nearly as reluctant anymore. Her resistance melted away as she let me pull her into me. "Okay, maybe one drink."

NINE

Ivy

I USUALLY PASSED on partying at Rainbow Central when Jenna asked, but I wanted to make an effort getting to know my new housemate.

The music was audible from out on the street and a cluster of people had gathered on the sidewalk. Giggling, chatting, dancing. The familiar smell of alcohol, mixed perfume, and cigarette smoke greeted us when we walked into the bar. By day, it was such a cosy and intimate place but by night, they really pulled out all the stops. The disco lights flashing through the place brought moments of connection in the otherwise unrecognisable mass of people and illuminated the bar where two servers were diligently working. Frances and the girls from her party were immediately recognised upon entry and greeted what felt like at least twenty of thirty people under the pink crest of their student club, Platypus. I stood by awkwardly, feeling out of place like always. It wasn't like the people here weren't welcoming, on the contrary, but I always felt like a fraud infiltrating a sacred space. Maybe that was silly, but I could tell the way girls looked at me, and I felt like an imposter when I told them I was straight. Didn't that defeat the point of them gathering in one place?

While they were all greeting each other, I made my way over to the bar to get another drink. A little unsteady on my feet, I almost bumped into a girl with raven hair waiting to get the server's attention.

"Oh, carefully there." She steadied me with a big smile. "Or you'll fall for me."

I laughed at her dorky pick-up line. "Does that line ever work for you?"

"Only on the cute ones." She leaned in so she didn't have to shout over the music. "What are you drinking?"

"Rosé. Or I might get one of those cocktails, they look yummy."

"The Rainbow Central one is really good."

"Oh, I had that last time. It's very nice."

She looked me up and down appreciatively. "So you're a regular? I haven't seen you before."

"No, no. Not a regular."

"Shame." She waved at the passing bartender. "Nini! Two Rainbow Centrals."

"Oh no, you don't need to buy me a drink," I quickly said but it was too late.

The other girl handed her card over the bar and passed me one of the cocktails. The cold glass was slick with condensation and to bridge the awkward tension, held out the money for the drink. "Here."

"No, no, it's my treat."

"I don't need to be treated," I countered, placing the money on the bar. I knew what social contract a drink really was and I didn't like it when random guys bought me drinks hoping to get lucky later, I didn't need it from women either.

The other girl chuckled as she reluctantly accepted the money. "Alright. Independent. I like that."

I checked the crowd for Frances. "I've got to go back to my friends."

"I'll help you find them." The other girl stuck by my side. "I'm Melania. What's your name?"

"Ivy," I answered.

"Ivy. That's cute."

"Thanks." I spotted Frances hugging one of her

friends and I waved to get her attention. The sea of people prevented me from catching her eye so I pushed through a group of dancing guys and swerved around two girls making out. By the time I got to where Frances was standing, another girl was taking up her attention and I didn't want to steal her away.

"Hey, Ivy!" someone called. An arm was wrapped around my shoulder and I looked up to see Tash, one of Frances' friends from before. "Where did you go?"

"I was buying a drink," I replied, glancing at Melania who seemed annoyed that someone interrupted us.

Tasha chuckled as she pulled me towards the spot where some of the others from before had gathered, already dancing and swaying to the music. I checked if Melania was following but she seemed to have given up and had returned to the bar.

I turned to Tasha and breathed a sigh of relief. "Thank you!"

"You looked like you needed rescuing," she shouted back, bopping along to the music.

"How did you know?"

"Ahh, Melania is always on the prowl. She can't resist fresh meat. Ooooh, Erin! Over here!" She waved at a girl entering, bouncing to her with an energy that made people step out of the way, and the two embraced with a kiss.

So that had to be the girlfriend. Frances had so many friends, it was hard to keep up with who was who, but I was getting the hang of it.

Tasha ushered the new girl back and the group welcomed her with screaming excitement. Everyone hugged and kissed and greeted her like she was the prodigal daughter returning home. Except they greeted everyone they knew like this.

I waited on the outskirts of the group, feeling a little left out. I thought I was drunk enough for this but the walk here sobered me up quite a bit and it was just becoming painfully obvious how few people I knew.

Maybe I should've stuck to my guns and stayed home but Frances had just been too convincing.

I took a big sip from my cocktail and tried to get in a dancing mood. The music was good and I wanted to surrender to the hypnotic beat pounding through the place. I swayed back and forth, quietly singing along to the song. If only Jenna was here, I wouldn't feel so out of place, but occasionally, she did have other plans than partying at her student club.

Something tapped me on the shoulder and I opened my eyes, surprised to find Frances standing in front of me. She had her arm wrapped around Tasha's girlfriend and wrapped her other around me, pulling her close. "Ivy! This is Erin, she's Tash's girl."

I smiled. "I figured."

"Erin, this is my new roommate."

The other girl clapped her hands before pulling me into a hug. "Awww, nice to meet you!"

Surprised by the warm greeting, I hugged her back somewhat half-heartedly. "Nice to meet you too."

"Hey, I recognise you. Aren't you Jenna's friend?"

I nodded. "Yeah, she's my best friend."

"Ahh, I thought you looked familiar. Small world," she noted. Someone else waved at her and with a quick apology, she bounced away, leaving me with Frances.

The tall girl took a step closer, virtually towering over me. "Hey, you okay?"

I nodded. "Yeah, just feeling a bit tired already."

"I know how to fix that," she responded, the twinkle in her eyes predicting nothing good.

"I dread to ask."

"Jager booooombs!" she shouted. Her friends around her cheered and if possible, got even more hyped.

I started protesting until I realised it was futile. Everyone around me was chanting 'shots' and Tasha and Erin had already gone off to buy what I could only assume would be a platter of them. Oh dear.

Suspiciously quick, they returned with a ridiculous amount of shots and passed them around the group of people. At least this was an easy way of figuring out who was part of their friend group and who wasn't. I thought about passing on the shot but seeing everyone with a shot, I didn't want to brand myself like an outsider.

I accepted the little cool glass, already able to smell the anise and the rest of the strong spices. It wasn't my favourite drink by any means but hopefully, the energy drink in there would perk me right up.

"To my new flat!" Frances shouted, raising her glass. "And to Ivy, my new roommate. Cheers!"

I was taken off guard by at least ten people shouting my name and quickly threw the jager bomb back, trying not to cough as the alcohol burned a way down my throat. That wasn't exactly pleasant but needs must.

The music changed and a new song came on, one I actually recognised. Frances pulled me towards her and her contagious smile got me in a better mood in no time. I surrendered to the atmosphere, tuning in with the sway of the crowd and letting the haze of the alcohol set in.

After dancing for a good hour with Frances and her friends, and having had a couple more drinks, I felt confident enough to pull away from the group for some fresh air. The later it got, the more people were gathering on the sidewalk. Everyone was still chatting and smoking, but the number of people making out had gone up.

I picked a spot to the side of the large window to sit down, wishing I'd left my heels at home. This was going to hurt tomorrow.

A voice called my name and I looked up, expecting to see one of Frances' mates. Wrong. A familiar face joined me on the step and shot me an objectively charming smile.

"Hey. Melania, right?"

She grinned. "You remembered."

"Yeah." I glanced past her at the rest of the people outside, hoping to recognise someone, but no dice. "How's your evening?"

"Great, I love dancing." She raised her arms and moved to the faint beat inside. "And all the beautiful women."

"Right."

"So you're Tash's friend?"

I shook my head. "No, Frances is my new roommate."

"Ooh, I see. Well, Frances is lucky," she winked

conspiringly, like we were old buddies that shared multiple secrets. She pulled a packet of cigarettes from her shirt's breast pocket and held one out to me. "Smoke?"

"No, I don't smoke."

"Me neither, I just carry these around in case I meet a cute girl," she said, putting the packet away. The faint smell of cigarettes on her made it pretty obvious that was a lie. There was only one reason why people lied on a night out. To get laid. That was the most common reason, at least.

Maybe it was presumptuous to assume she was flirting and wasn't just trying to be friendly but nobody was this persistent when trying to make friends. She should've taken the hint when I paid her back for the cocktail but they never did, did they?

"Hi, listen. I don't want to make assumptions and you seem very friendly, but I'm not—"

"Iiiiiiivy!" A second figure plopped down on the other side of me and swung their arm around me. "I've been wondering where you went. What are you doing out here?"

"Getting some fresh air." Relieved to no longer be on my own with Melania, I leaned into Frances' embrace. Even though we'd only known each other for a short while, I felt safe with her. If she was going to try something nefarious, she'd do it in the confines of our own home, not in a busy club.

She patted my head affectionately. "You a little tipsy?"

"Little bit."

With a chuckle, she tickled my nose. "You're such a lightweight."

I gave her a little nudge. "Hey! That's your fault with your bombs and your wine and your smile."

"My smile? Why is my smile to blame?"

I poked her cheek. "It's too cute."

"You *are* drunk," she laughed, revealing her two dimples.

"There." I pointed at them. "There's the cuteness."

"These old things?" She grabbed her cheeks and pulled on them, moving them while she spoke.

A laugh bubbled up from my gut as we joked and chatted. At some point, I realised Melania had left but I didn't notice until she was gone.

I rested my head on Frances' shoulder, enjoying the night's cool air. "I'm tired."

"I'm not surprised. I think it's time I take you home. The party is pretty much over anyway."

"Thanks. Sorry to be a drag."

"You're not a drag."

I hiccuped. "I'm sure Melania doesn't agree."

"Ah, don't worry about her. She's shameless."

"I feel… bad. I know it's silly but this is a rainbow bar. I don't have any business here. Isn't the point that you can come here and don't have to worry whether someone is or isn't into girls?"

"No, the point is for us to have fun. Don't feel bad about rejecting her. Or anyone else, for that matter. You're not a piece of meat that they're entitled to. Even if you were into women, you might not have been into her so what's the difference? Not interested is not interested."

Her logic made a lot of sense, maybe because I was tipsy, but I felt relieved regardless. "That's a good point."

"I'm clever, aren't I?" She teased, pushing herself up. She held out her hand. "Come on, let's go home."

I happily took her hand and let her pull me up from the step. My wobbly legs gave in and I collided with her. Luckily, she steadied me as the hazy world turned around me.

She chuckled, her breath warm on my skin. And that was the last thing I remembered.

TEN

Ivy

MORNING CAME with a hammering headache and a swirling stomach. A loud, hammering noise penetrated through my skull. How could my headache be this loud?

The noise continued and it took me a moment to work out it was my phone vibrating on the nightstand. One glance at the screen had me groaning. Why now?

I picked up Mum's call, already dreading the lectures and faux-life lessons she was going to give me. "Hi, Mum."

"Hello, lemon drop. It's been a while. How are you?"

With a sigh, I sat down on my bed. "It's not been that long, we spoke like two weeks ago."

"That's a long time for me. So what's new in your life? I saw a picture of you on that website, what's it called... FaceView? Did you gain weight again?"

Gah, I knew she was going to ask. She always did, just making me feel even more insecure about my body.

Mum didn't wait for an answer. "How's Jenna? Did she finally move in with her lesbian girlfriend?"

"You can just say girlfriend, you don't need to add lesbian," I corrected like always. If I could've rolled my eyes out of their sockets, I would've.

"But then how do people know they're lesbians? She's your girlfriend too."

"Girl friend," I emphasised the pause, stretching it out longer than necessary. "Girl. Friend. Or best friend would work too."

"Right. Anyway, do you remember Dianne Wieling from down the street? I ran into her yesterday at the grocer and she said her niece is looking for a place to rent in the city. Maybe she could move in to replace your girlfriend."

"Girl friend," I grumbled. "And there's no need, Frances moved in a couple of days ago."

"Oh my, why didn't you tell me you finally found a boyfriend? What's his name, Francis? Tell me all about him, is he handsome? Does he cook? Is he a polite young man? Bring him over for lunch this weekend, I want to meet him!"

"No, Frances, Mum. Frances with an E."

"So he's French?"

"No, Frances is a girl's name."

"Ooooh. *Oh.* Oh, I see. Well, I didn't expect to hear about it this way but I can't say I'm surprised. You were always so close with Jenna."

It took me a moment to figure out what she was saying. "No, no, no. Mum, it's not like that. She's just a—"

"As long as you're happy! I'm just glad you've finally found someone. You know, a mother's greatest worry is that her daughter is going to end up with some awful husband or worse, alone. I've been worried about you. When I was your age, I was already married and expecting you. But finally!"

The misunderstanding just kept growing but any attempt to correct her was overridden by her speech.

"I want you to know that your father and I love you no matter what. You be bold and brave, sweetheart. Love who you want to love. We're so proud of you." It sounded like she was tearing up. The line crackled as she muffled the speaker and I could hear her shout across the room. "Walt! Walter! Our little Ivy has finally found herself love!"

"Tell her to bring her new boyfriend over for dinner!" my father shouted back, probably from his reclining chair on the other side of the living room with a cold beer in one hand and engrossed in his newspaper.

"It's a lesbian girlfriend, Walt! Get with the times!" Mum hollered across the room.

Despite the misunderstanding and their outdated views, I felt affectionate towards my parents. They were trying and it was good to know that if I'd been a lesbian, they'd have treated me just the same. I was thankful for that. I just wish she'd let me explain that Frances was just a roommate, nothing else. Although it would make my life easier if they thought I was in a relationship. Then they'd finally stop nagging or trying to set me up with one of their friends' sons.

Yeah. Maybe this misunderstanding wasn't so bad. It wasn't like Frances had to even know about it, it would just be something to keep my parents off my back. A little white lie so they stopped pretending my life was a Greek tragedy because I dropped out of school and had no boyfriend and no job prospects.

"We'd love to meet Frances. You should bring her

along this weekend so we can get to know this young lady," Mum said in her stern voice.

"I'll check if she's free but probably not, she's very busy," I lied sweetly. My stomach churned from last night's indulgence and I muffled a little burp. Oh, oh. "Mum, I got to go, I'll see you this weekend, okay? Byeee."

"Byeee, honey poo."

I hung up, cutting off her smooching sounds, and got up to find something for my stomach. Hangovers were the worst. While I was fixing myself a glass of water in the kitchen, I heard Frances' door open.

"Hey Ivy?" She sat down at the kitchen table, her eyebrows knitted together in a frown. "Is there a reason why your mum posted on my wall with: 'Welcome to the family, can't wait to meet you Sunday.' What's Sunday?"

I froze. "What?"

"I think it's your mum. Look." She tilted her phone towards me.

It took just a glance at the screen to confirm my worst nightmare and I facepalmed my forehead. "Gah. I'm so sorry, I can't believe she did that."

"Want to explain? Why is she welcoming me to the family?"

I sat down opposite of her, taking a sip of my

water. "Okay so… Don't take this the wrong way but I might've told my parents a little lie. Or I guess, I didn't correct a misunderstanding. When I was telling them about my new roommate, she assumed you were my boyfriend. When I said you were a girl, she thought I meant you were my girlfriend. She's always on my case about finding a man and she sounded so happy I found someone. I thought maybe I could escape the holiday grilling about why I'm single. So stupid, I should've known that wasn't going to work."

My roommate thought for a moment. "What's Sunday?"

"She invited us over for lunch but I'll just have to tell her she misunderstood."

"Maybe you don't."

I frowned. "What do you mean?"

With a shrug, she shot me a look. "I'm not doing anything on Sunday."

"Really? You want to go to my parents and pretend to be my girlfriend?" I frowned. "Why?"

"I'm bored and it'll help you out, right?"

"Yes…"

"Then why not?" Frances tapped her phone screen and smiled. "Oh, hey. What are the rules for decorating the flat? It's almost Christmas and all we've got is Santa Bear."

I looked at the cardboard cut-out and as always, smiled at the sight of the bear with the Christmas hat. "We can do whatever you want as long as you don't want me to do anything today."

"No worries, I'm a little hungover too." Frances thought for a moment. "Can we have lights?"

"Sure."

"Real tree?"

"Yes, I hate fake ones. Nothing better than that real pine smell," I mused, inhaling deeply.

"Totally agree, I love decorating trees. I've got loads of adorable ornaments and baubles. Oh, how about a wreath at the door?"

I chuckled, her enthusiasm contagious. "Whatever you want."

"I see, being your fake-girlfriend immediately comes with perks, huh?" she teased, shooting me a wink.

"You bet," I joked back, not against a little bit of friendly flirting. Especially if we were going to pretend to be a couple, it would sell the ruse. Although pretending to have chemistry with Frances wasn't going to be hard. There was just something about her that made me want to spend time with her.

ELEVEN

Frances

WHY WAS I feeling nervous when I knew this wasn't a real meet-the-parents? What if this ruined our budding friendship? What if it completely fucked up our housemate arrangement? I'd only just moved in, I didn't want to go through the trouble of finding a new place again. Damn it, why had I said yes again?

I parked the car in the neat driveway and turned to Ivy, not able to shake off my worries. "What if your parents don't believe we're a couple? What if they want us to kiss?"

Ivy chuckled. "They're not the kiss-police. We don't have to give them a relationship certificate, just you showing up here will be convincing enough. And you know, if they want to see a kiss, we'll just give each other a little kiss, right?"

I wasn't sure if I heard that right. I stared at the woman next to me, trying to decipher if this was a trap or not. "So you wouldn't mind kissing me? Ivy Daniels, if you wanted to make out with me, you didn't have to make up a fake relationship."

She laughed as she got out of the car. "Oh, yes. I've made up this elaborate lie just to get a snog."

"Can't say I'm complaining that I'll be the first girl you kiss," I teased, clutching my chest dramatically. "Don't get me wrong, it's a grave burden but it's a sacrifice I'm willing to make."

She snorted as she opened the door. "You're going to get on great with my dad. Shall we?"

"I'll try my best. Any skeletons in the closet I should know about?" I asked as we walked up the stone path. The front garden was nicely kept and had that homely touch that made me believe they took care of their yard themselves, instead of hiring a gardener.

Ivy thought for a moment as we skipped the front door and continued on to the back. "Don't say anything about hot air balloons. Don't mention my older brother, Steven. Oh, and not a word about Mum's awful green beans."

"Duly noted." I sighed dramatically. "The things I do for fake-love."

She jabbed her elbow in my ribs. "Shh, not so loud."

I giggled nervously. "Sorry."

Before Ivy opened the back door, I grabbed her by the wrist and pulled her back, pressing her against the side of the house. "Hang on."

"What?"

"Are you sure about this? You really want to lie to your family?"

Ivy sighed. "I know it's kind of weird but you don't know them like I do. They're obsessed with my happiness and after I dropped out of school, I'm sure they think I'm a lost cause."

"Okay, it's your family." I stepped out of her private space and put my hands in my pockets, trying to calm myself. Even though it wasn't real, it was still nerve-wracking to meet parents.

Before we entered the house, Ivy paused, her hand on the doorknob. "Oh, and what makes you think this is my first time kissing a girl?"

The mischievous twinkle in her eyes turned my mouth dry and I chased after her, cursing her perfect timing as we stepped into her parents' kitchen and I was forced to swallow any remarks about her comment. Damn that girl, she really knew how to press my buttons. I'd get her back for that, somehow. But first, I had to play the doting girlfriend.

Ivy opened the door and a lovely, homely smell greeted us. A woman that looked like an older version of her came towards us and pulled her into a hug. "Lemon drop! You made it. Ahh, it's so good to see you. Oh, looks like you've put on some weight."

She released her daughter and approached me with open arms. "You must be Frances! It's so nice to meet you."

She pulled me into such a tight, welcoming hug, I felt my bones creak. She released me after a moment or two and sized me up. "You're tall."

"Thank you?"

"Like a model," she clarified.

"Ah. Thank you."

She turned around and patted Ivy's back. "Our little Ivy has a nice face but she likes food a little too much to be a model, huh?"

"Mum!"

"I think Ivy has a great figure," I defended her, earning a grateful smile from her.

She mouthed a thank you as she moved to take my jacket. "Where's Dad?"

"In the living room reading his newspaper, where else?" She grabbed the jackets from Ivy and draped them over her arm. "Go take a seat, dinner is almost ready. You want anything to drink?"

"Tea is alright," Ivy responded, turning to me. "You?"

"Umm, same."

Ivy's mother nodded. "Alright, let me put these coats away and I'll brew you a cup."

I smiled. "Thanks, Mrs Daniels."

"You're welcome, dear. And call me Martha."

"Thanks, Martha." I caught Ivy's eye as we made our way to the living room, hoping she didn't regret bringing me yet. Even though we weren't romantically involved, I wanted to make a good impression on my housemate's parents.

We entered the cosy living room that looked nothing like the one in my parents' house. Instead of uncomfortable furniture that was mostly for show, a man that I presumed was Ivy's father sat in an old, dingy chair that had years of wear and tear on it. He was rocking back and forth as he read his newspaper and listened to some soft music, with a large tiger cat curled around his feet.

"Hey, Dad. Hey, Millie!" Ivy greeted as she went over to kiss her father's cheek and patted the cat.

"Ahh, my little Ivy." He folded his newspaper into two and put it away so he could greet her warmly. "So good to see you. How are you?"

She smiled. "I'm good."

"You sure? Do you have enough money? Life is expensive nowadays. I just read that some billionaire bought a lot in Sapphire Bay for literal millions. Houses shouldn't cost that much."

She patted his arm. "I'm doing alright, Dad, don't worry about me. And they're not exactly building houses over there, are they?"

"I suppose not," he grumbled. "Did you have a good trip?"

She nodded as we sat down on the large couch. "Yes, Frances drove."

"I see." Her father turned his eye to me. "So you've got a car?"

I nodded. "I do, sir. I don't get much use out of it in the city but it's handy to have."

"Ah, call me Walt. And I remember when I got my first car. It was this dirty old pick-up truck that rattled everywhere I drove but oh, I loved that thing. Drove it when I took Martha on our first date. We conceived our little Ivy in the back of it too, not on the first date though."

Ivy flushed red. "Daaaad! Oh my god, why do you have to tell everyone?"

"What? I'm proud of that night, we made you. Why can't I tell people? It's not like it's a secret your mum and I did it. You're here, aren't you? You can count backwards from your birthday."

She pressed her hands against her ears. "Aaah, I don't want to hear it."

I couldn't hold back my chuckle. We'd only been here for five minutes and both her parents already embarrassed her. Even if she didn't like it, at least they knew her well enough to tease her. At least now I knew where she got her oversharing from.

TWELVE

Frances

Before Ivy's father could tell more about his magical night, Martha returned from the kitchen with a tray with a pot of tea and colourful mugs. She put them down on the coffee table and Ivy passed one to me.

"No crabs on this one," I muttered to her.

"What? Crabs? Oh! Frances, shh!" She shot me a glare but I could see the amusement flicking in her eyes.

There, that was three for three on the teasing front. I shuffled a little closer to her, like I would if I was madly in love with her, and draped one arm over the back of the couch, somewhat cuddling her. It felt really awkward and wrong so I quickly pulled it back, not before Ivy shot me a knowing grin.

Martha disappeared again, no doubt to finish cooking, and Walt happily chat with Ivy about everything and nothing. Even after only being here for a little bit, it was already overwhelmingly clear that they loved her. I didn't really understand why she felt the need to lie to them but of course, I didn't know what they were like when she was on her own. It wasn't really my place to judge, I was just here as a favour to a friend. And the home-cooked meal.

"Lunch is ready!" Martha's voice came from the kitchen.

Walt groaned as he got up from his chair. "Ah, my damn back."

"You okay, Dad?" Ivy asked, rushing over to give him a hand.

He waved her concerns away. "Yeah, yeah, don't you worry about your old man. That's just the price of life. And your mum's bloody thrift-shopping. You know, last week she found this ginormous cabinet. Solid oak. Almost broke my back getting that thing in the van but at least we made a tidy profit after she restored it. But that's marriage for you. Maybe that's something you'll get to experience soon, huh?"

"Dad! Frances and I only just started dating," Ivy lied as they continued on to the kitchen.

Their bickering made me smile. It was so different from the cool and distant interactions I had with my parents, it made me feel nostalgic for something I never had.

I waited for all of them to sit down and took the last seat at the table, not wanting to accidentally steal someone's spot.

Martha put multiple steaming pots down with ladles and large serving spoons. "Help yourself."

Not used to this kind of casual dinner, I checked with Ivy for guidance. Sensing my awkwardness, she filled my plate for me and helped herself after.

"So what do your parents do, Frances?" Martha inquired as we all dug in.

I'd been expecting this question yet it took me off guard. "Umm, well. My dad is in real estate, mostly commercial sites. And Mum gives lectures all over the world."

"Impressive. What does she teach?"

"Self-care," I noted bitterly, the irony not escaping me. All her preaching about empowerment and feminism was just her excuse to do whatever she wanted without having to take me into consideration.

Martha smiled as she ate a green bean. "I recently

read a great book about self-care. Who was it by, let me think… Ah, Elizabeth Woodson. She's a queen."

My smile soured. "That's Mum."

"Your mum is Elizabeth Woodson?" Ivy chimed in, earning surprised looks from her parents. "I didn't know that."

"I don't really like telling people." I reached out to touch her hand. "Sorry, I should've told you. You're my girlfriend after all."

She smiled reassuringly. "It's okay, we've got all the time in the world to get to know each other."

I knew that was a line straight out of a cheesy rom-com and I fully intended to tease her about that later.

The evening passed quickly with loads of stories being shared back and forth and the warm chatter at the table lingered long after we drove home, the Christmas jingles softly playing in the background. After parking the car and going up the stairs, I unlocked the door, careful not to knock the wreath off.

"Finally home," Ivy sighed as she fell down on the couch. "I love my parents but they exhaust me."

I chuckled as I sat down next to her. "Come on, that wasn't so bad. They were really friendly and they totally seemed to believe we were a couple."

"Yes. I'm so glad. That'll hopefully get them off

my back until the holidays, at least. I know they seemed all nice and everything, but I promise, they've been hounding me about missing out on love."

"Well, I'm happy to have helped. Fake-girlfriend," I said, shooting her a playful wink. I continued on in an exaggerated, teasing voice. "Although I must say, I'm very disappointed I didn't get at least one kiss."

Ivy laughed. "See, I told you, no kissing police."

"Luckily. So as your fake-girlfriend, do I have any claim over your mum's leftovers?"

"You actually liked her food?" she asked, sounding surprised.

"Yeah, it was great. You can really tell it's homemade."

"Wow, I'll have to tell her that. She'll be glad to hear, we're not always the biggest fans."

I managed a smile. "My family doesn't do much cooking so it was a real treat for me."

"Aww, I'm sorry to hear that. Are you not close?"

I shrugged, my gaze fixated on the Christmas tree in the corner of the flat. If I focused on one of the baubles, I could see my reflection in it. "Not really. They were always busy working and they're sickeningly in love. I always feel like the third wheel. Did I tell you they'll be on a cruise over my birthday?"

Ivy gently touched my knee. "I'm sorry to hear that."

"Yeah. That's just Mum and Dad. They're always off on adventures of their own."

"When's your birthday?" she inquired.

"In ten days. I'm turning twenty-three, if you can believe it."

Her eyes twinkled. "We should throw a party."

"What? No, don't be silly. It's a Wednesday, you've got work the next day."

"I can call and change my hours. We have to celebrate!"

I was touched by her consideration but I didn't expect her to change her schedule just for me. I was sure she'd have forgotten next week anyway so I just smiled and nodded. "Sure."

"Great. We'll invite all your friends over and go clubbing or something?"

"Yeah, sounds fun."

"Awesome." She yawned and rotated her neck. "Oof, I'm tired. I think I need some rest."

"Me too," I admitted. "It was fun meeting your parents but that was a lot of peopling."

"You're telling me." She got up from the couch and stretched again. "Ahhh. I guess I'll see you tomorrow?"

I rose too, my body protesting from all the sitting. "Yup. I don't have class so I'm sleeping in."

"Yeah, I'm off too."

The prospect made me smile. I yawned as I stepped away from the couch, the sleep making my body heavy. "Alright, night."

"Oh, hey?" With a twinkle in her eyes, she skipped towards me and pressed up on the tips of her toes. Her mouth was on mine before I could even fully process what was happening or react. She pulled back from the kiss, leaving me breathless and with tingling lips.

I drew a shaky breath. "What was that for?"

"To combat your disappointment," she teased, repeating my words from earlier. "Thanks for going with me today. I really appreciate it."

"Hey, what are housemates for?"

She laughed. "Not this, I don't think. Anyway, night night, Frances."

My mouth was all dried up as she made her way to her room, leaving me a little lost and confused in the living room. I reached up to touch my lips, taken aback by how affected I was by her kiss.

I pushed my conflicted feelings back as I returned to my room and reminded myself of the rules. Roommate, straight.

"Don't go there," I muttered to myself as I closed the door, trying to forget the kiss. It had been a thank-you, a kiss between friends, a meaningless little kiss. Nothing to obsess over.

Roommate. Straight. Roommate. Straight.

THIRTEEN

Ivy

DID I go too far by kissing her? In the heat of the moment, it seemed like a funny thing to do but now that I was in bed, I was worried about the implications. Would Frances think I was making a pass at her?

I turned on my side, throwing my blanket off.

It had been a nice kiss, but it was barely more than a peck. A quick smooch between friends. The fake-girlfriend thing complicated it a little but it was *fake.* Fake.

My toes got cold and I adjusted my duvet, bunching it up so I could kind of straddle it.

Why did I kiss her? Whyyyyy. If she'd been a guy, I wouldn't have unless I was into him. But she wasn't a guy and kissing girls was different anyway. I'd kissed Jenna plenty of times for fun on a drunken night out and those never meant anything.

Gah, this was ridiculous. I was overthinking this. Frances was a sensible girl, she probably knew it meant nothing. But it wasn't fair to give her mixed signals so I had to be a little more careful. Surely, everything would be better when I woke up. At least, that was what I told myself as I fell asleep.

The fever dreams and the gnawing worry in the morning told a different story. After a night of tossing and turning, I got up earlier than usual. Trying to sleep wasn't making me feel better and knowing Frances wouldn't be up at this hour meant I could enjoy some worry-free coffee.

I opened my door quieter than usual, peeking out to make sure the flat was empty. I made sure I could hear light snoring through my roommate's door before I tiptoed to the kitchen and turned the coffee machine on.

After inserting the filter and filling the tank, I reached for the colourful tin that we kept the ground coffee in.

Empty.

Of course, the one time I wanted to be sneaky, I had to ground new beans.

"Tea, it is," I muttered to myself, flicking the kettle on instead and reaching for my favourite mug. The painted dandelions on them always brightened my morning and it made every beverage taste better.

While I poured the boiling water on my teabag, a noise startled me and I jumped, almost burning myself. "Fuck!"

"Are you okay?" Frances' voice was thick from sleep but the concern was easily detectable. She rushed over to me, almost tripping over her bathrobe ribbon.

Worried, I turned and mug in hand, smacked it against the side. The porcelain shattered and the hot water gushed out the cracks, clattering to the stone floor and spilling onto my feet.

"Double fuck!" I jumped back just in time to avoid any serious injury. There went my favourite mug. Ugh, what a disastrous morning.

Frances avoided the spill and pushed the table and chairs to the side so the tea water wouldn't get to them. "What are you doing?"

"Trying to make tea," I grumbled.

"Why were you being so loud?"

I pulled my usual chair out and sank down on it,

head in hands. "I'm sorry if I woke you. I was actually trying to be quiet."

"Did you know most people make more noise when they're trying to be silent than if they were just going about their usual business?" Frances commented.

"Is that true?"

She sat down on her chair, shrugging as she turned towards me. "I don't know, I'm teasing."

"Oh, it's a joke." I chuckled tersely. "Ha, funny. Yeah."

"Why aren't you having coffee?"

"Umm, I was feeling too lazy to grind more coffee," I lied, getting up to clean the spillage and put more distance between us. I mopped up the water with a rag and picked up the pieces of my mug. So much for it brightening my day.

Frances handed me the dustpan, helpful as always. I quickly crouched down again, not wanting to look her in the eye. What if I really messed everything up? What if she thought that kiss meant more than it did? What if she tried to kiss me this time?

"Shall we try that again?" Frances suggested as she filled the kettle with more water.

"If you're awake, maybe I'll grind that coffee after

all," I said, reaching for the pouch of beans. "Oh, we're almost out of these too."

"We should buy some new ones. Better ones. There's a cute little shop in town where they sell all kinds of fair-trade coffee beans that have a lot more character."

I filled up the grinder, happy to have my back towards her. "Sounds expensive."

"I promise it's worth the price."

The scraping sounds behind me told me she was putting the table and chairs back into place and when I turned around, everything was pretty as a picture again. Especially Frances. Despite her morning hair and her loose pyjamas, she was looking a whole lot better than me without make-up.

I finished making the coffee, aware of the tense silence hanging in the kitchen. Every passing second just added to the growing elephant in the room. She *had* to be thinking about this too, right?

With a smile plastered on my face, I put one of the mugs of coffee on the table, matching up the bottom with the checkers on the table cloth. "Here's yours. I'm going to drink mine in my room, bye."

I'd made it halfway across the flat when Frances called my name.

Frozen, I took a moment before I turned around. "Yes?"

"Something going on?"

I shook my head. "No, no. I'm… meeting up with Jenna so I need to get dressed."

"You're sure there's nothing else?"

With a gulp, I shrugged. "No, should there be?"

Frances' intense gaze lingered on me. "No."

"Okay. See you later then." I rushed to my room, quickly closing the door behind me. My heart was pounding in my chest and I released a miserable sigh. I hated lying but what was I supposed to say?

Oh, I knew. I put my mug down and grabbed my phone from my nightstand. If I met up with Jenna, it was only technically a lie. *What are you doing this morning?*

My phone vibrated almost immediately with Jenna's response. *Advanced chem. Booooored to death. Why?*

I grinned, relieved she was awake. *Want to go shopping?*

Defo. I can be at our bench in twenty.

See you there. Relieved, I tossed my phone on my bed and got dressed to meet up with my best friend. Maybe it was a little pathetic to flee my own flat but I'd created this situation, it was only fair that I dealt with it.

When I stepped out of my room, the flat was empty. Frances' door was closed but I couldn't tell if she was in there or had left. The empty mug in the sink didn't give me more information so I just took the win and got out.

Even though Christmas was still two weeks away, the city was fully decorated with all kinds of lights and snowflakes. Every store had a tree and wrapped gifts in the window, with big holiday discounts at the front. It truly transformed the city.

I met Jenna on our usual bench at the church square, happy to see her again.

"Daniels!" She waved as she rushed through the sparse crowd and pulled me into a hug.

"What's up, Jacobs." I embraced her tight, happy to see my friend.

"Not much. Ah, I missed your face," she joked, giving me a gentle nudge. "I love living with Steph, don't get me wrong, but it's weird not seeing you every day."

"I know. I miss you too," I admitted as we set in motion. "Have you had breakfast yet?"

"Does a bag of popcorn count?"

I laughed. "No. Shall we stop by that sandwich bar?"

"Yes, good idea. Larissa said they have some new Christmas items on the menu."

"We waited by the lights and clicked my tongue. "Larissa... Isn't that the girl you had that summer fling with?"

"Depends on which summer you're talking about," Jenna joked as we crossed the street. "But yes. Great sex, but that was it."

"Do you know every lesbian in town?" I asked in mock-exasperation.

"Pretty much," she beamed.

We continued on, weaving through the handful of people out and about. For a student city, the mornings were usually pretty quiet with mostly older people braving the streets. Grey clouds hung over the square and the crisp morning helped clear my head.

The sandwich bar we frequented often was cosy and calm, a cute bistro that really suited the atmosphere of the city. We ordered breakfast, not without some awful and cringy flirting between Jenna and her ex-fling, but at least it got us a discount.

We wandered back to the church square, chatting about nothing and everything. It was hard to believe we'd only become best friends a couple of years ago but there was a kind of closeness that could only be achieved by living with someone.

"Oh, before we eat, let's take a selfie," I suggested,

whipping out my phone.

Jenna seemed confused but shuffled closer. I centered us in the frame and snapped a couple of quick shots. With the pictures done, I dug into my sandwich.

"Ooh, this is so good," Jenna moaned.

"It is. Can I ask a question?" I asked with a mouthful of salami.

Jenna nodded. "Shoot."

"How do you know the difference between say, Larissa and me."

My best friend's eyebrows shot up. "That's an interesting question. What do you mean?"

"Well... How do you decide whether someone is going to become a friend or more?"

"Chemistry."

"We have chemistry," I pointed out.

"Not that kind of chemistry. Attraction," Jenna shrugged. "Don't you know whether you're drawn to a guy or not?"

"I guess?"

"It's the same for me." She finished her sandwich and crumpled up the paper into a ball. "Although truth be told, I'm pretty much down for whoever is into me. It's a small pond so I'll take whatever I can catch. Doesn't mean I don't throw some back. That's what I did until I met Steph."

I nodded, trying to make sense of what she was saying. "So you're saying we're friends because I'm not into you?"

"Kind of. If I were single and you wanted more, I'd be up for trying it. But only because we're close. I wouldn't say yes to just anyone."

Her answer surprised me. "Even if it ruined our friendship?"

"I think not trying would ruin our friendship more. There'd be this unspoken imbalance that would eat away at us and eventually, things would break. Relationships are about honesty, right? I already tell you everything so why would that change?" She studied me for a moment, her strong eyebrows knitted together. "What's this about? Are you saying you want us to get together?"

"No, gosh, no. Sorry, just a thought experiment."

Jenna released a deep sigh. "Thank god." So what *is* this about? Are you having your own lesbian awakening? Is someone opening up your flower? Got the urge to merge vaginas?"

I pretended to barf. "Gross, why would you put it like that?"

She laughed. "I don't know, I've never said any of those things before. But seriously, something going on? Maybe with you and Frances?"

"No, nothing like that. I'm just trying to figure

out where the boundaries are in terms of girl closeness. I don't want to give her the wrong impression."

Jenna patted my shoulder reassuringly. "Just talk to her. I don't know her that well but she's a cool chick. Look, there are three types of lesbians. We've got those who will flirt aggressively with anything and anyone. If she was interested, you'd know. Two, the ones who will literally never tell you they're into you. They never make any moves so if you're not interested, it won't go anywhere."

I picked my lip, my gaze focused on a pigeon scouring for crumbs. "And the third kind?"

"The useless kind. Is terrible at flirting, doesn't get hints. They're just oblivious."

"Those are some strong stereotypes."

"Hey, they're stereotypes for a reason. Now I'm not saying everyone is like that but from what I've seen from Frances, she's usually pretty flirty and friendly. If she's not making the moves, she's probably not interested."

"Interesting." I ran every interaction I'd had with my new roommate through my head, trying to figure out whether there had been anything I'd overlooked, but I came up blank. "Guess I'm worried for no reason then."

At least, I hoped so.

FOURTEEN

Frances

I KNEW Ivy was going to be freaked out by that kiss, even though she initiated it. Probably because she initiated it. If she'd stuck around long enough this morning, I'd have told her she had nothing to worry about.

With a sigh, I nestled myself on the couch for a casual day of binge watching. Maybe it would take my mind off the weird tension between us, although I doubted it. It was pretty clear that she was trying to avoid me and unfortunately, this wasn't the first time something like that happened.

Straight girls could be so flighty.

I turned the tv on, picking a random show with not too many episodes, and settling in for hours of mediocre writing and acting. At least it would kill time.

Somewhere around episode seven, I heard the jingle of keys on the landing. I hadn't expected her back so soon but she did live here so…

I waited for the front door to open before I spoke.

"Hey," I said as casually as I could, not looking away from the tv.

"Hi."

I listened to the rustle of fabric as she took her jacket off and the clicking of her approaching footsteps. The couch dipped as she took a seat next to me and the urge to look at her was overwhelming. Stubbornly, I kept my attention on my show, even though I wasn't really watching.

Ivy shuffled back and forth. "What are you watching?"

"A flower competition. They give lots of handy tips for novices."

"Thinking of starting that weed garden after all?" she joked awkwardly.

I kept my composure. "No, don't worry. Just the coral. You had a good time out?"

"Yes, I grabbed breakfast with Jenna."

"I saw the pictures," I remarked, recalling the notification on my feed. "Looked like fun."

"It was. She's my best friend so… Yeah."

I hummed. "Aha."

The other girl fidgeted with one of the pillows, the growing tension clearly making her restless. I wished I could let it go on but I wasn't that heartless. With a sigh, I paused my show and turned to face her. "Is there something we need to talk about?"

"No," she answered quickly.

"You sure?"

"No," she squeaked. "Okay, truth time?"

I nodded. "Lay it on me."

"Alright. I'm worried I might've given you the wrong impression, you know, with that kiss yesterday."

I knew it. So I didn't imagine all that awkwardness this morning. I knew she was going to be weird about it.

Ivy patted the pillow nervously. "Say something."

"We're cool," I answered, trying to formulate my thoughts properly. "Look, it was just a kiss. It didn't mean anything, right?"

"No, it didn't."

"There you go." I kept my tone light and nonchalant, biting back some disappointment. I wasn't even sure why I was feeling that way, it wasn't like I wanted to date Ivy. It just… it was never fun to hear someone wasn't interested.

Ivy kept her gaze on me as she shuffled back and forth on the couch. "So we're okay?"

"Yes, unless you want to keep being this weird, skittish person."

She chuckled nervously. "No. I don't like feeling like this."

I gave her the shortest pat on the knee, not wanting her to get the wrong impression. "Then we're fine. Chill out."

FIFTEEN

Ivy

After our conversation, things quickly returned to how they used to be. The easy and friendly atmosphere was only spiked by my struggles to come up with a birthday gift. I wanted to get her something special and meaningful but I didn't know her quite well enough for that. Nonetheless, I didn't just want to buy her a bottle of impersonal alcohol.

With a sigh, I pulled the next job from the printer, the glossy paper still warm. I didn't usually pay much attention to what we were asked to do, but the azure blue coast caught my eye. The shiny paper added an extra quality to the ocean, making it even more realistic.

A thought sprung in my mind as I made my way back to the table where my boss was organising the orders. "Hey, Rick. Do you think I could print something?"

He looked up from his computer. "Print something? You're in luck, we happen to be a print shop."

I laughed sarcastically. "Ha ha. I know, but I just wasn't sure if you'd want me to put in an official order or…"

"Nah, just print it during your break or a lull or something. As long as you're not trying to print a curriculum's worth of textbooks."

"No, no, I'd like a poster." I nodded to the poster in my hands. "Like this one."

Rick chuckled. "One poster? Yeah, you can have one poster."

"Thank you."

Excited to have come up with a present, I searched the internet for a nice picture. One of the stock websites I used before had some kind of Holiday discount on their images so I bought one of a nice, blue ocean. I printed it out, happy I came up with something in the nick of time for her birthday tomorrow.

Come morning, I skipped out of my room with my present hidden behind my back.

"Morning," Frances called from behind the tv, still in her pyjamas and with a blanket wrapped around her.

I sat down next to her and with a flourish, I revealed the cardboard tube from behind my back. "Tadaa."

She looked surprised. "What's this?"

"Happy birthday."

She slowly accepted the tube. "You bought me something?"

"Yeah. No, kind of."

"Kind of?" She rattled it softly. "You *stole* me something?"

I laughed. "Just open it."

She popped the plastic top off and shook the rolled-up poster out. She smoothed it out on the coffee table, exposing the bright blue ocean on it.

I watched her intently, nervous for her reaction. "Tadaa…"

Frances shot me a bemused but confused smile. "Thanks, I think? I'm not going to lie, Ivy. I'm a little confused."

"It's for behind your tank. To make it look like your coral friends are in the ocean." When she didn't say anything, I kept rattling. "You know, like an optical illusion, kind of. I know it's silly and I did have my boss' permission to print it so I didn't buy it and I didn't steal it, he kind of gave it to me. But like, it's still my gift—"

"I love it. This is so thoughtful." Her voice caught as she stared at the poster. "Thank you, Ivy."

I wasn't sure why she sounded teary but it seemed in a good way. At least, I hoped so.

"I know it's not a very fancy gift but—"

"No, it's perfect." She sniffled but coughed it away. "Oh, a parcel arrived for you."

So that was the cardboard box on the coffee table. Curious, I ripped the packaging tape off and tore into the parcel. A clink of bottles surprised me as I pulled out one. "Gin? Oh, there's a note."

"What's it say?"

"Happy Birthday, Frances. Welcome to the family, from Martha and Walt. P.S. Ivy, give this to your girlfriend," I read out loud, handing the bottle to my roommate. "I mentioned it was your birthday in our call last week. They must've remembered."

"How sweet," Frances mumbled. Something of a sob escaped her and she quickly pressed her hands against her mouth. "I'm sorry, I don't know why I'm getting emotional. This is just... So thoughtful."

A little awkwardly but well-intentioned, I patted her back. "You can talk to me."

The other girl released a frustrated groan. "It's nothing, I'm being ridiculous and ungrateful."

"Why are you ungrateful?"

"Because I'm upset that my parents are on a cruise and just deposited some money in my bank accounts as a birthday gift. How stupid is that? Loads of people don't even get anything so I shouldn't complain."

I gently pulled her arms away, opening her up. "Hey, it's not stupid. It's not about the money, it's about the lack of consideration."

"Yeah, pretty much." She mustered a smile and patted my knee. "But I don't want to start my twenty-third year resenting my parents. I've got good friends, I'll be alright."

"Yeah and my family is very welcoming."

She released her first genuine chuckle. "Yes, very. It's a good thing I like gin. Shall we crack into this bad boy? Get a drink before the party committee arrives."

"It's eleven in the morning," I pointed out.

"Coffee first then?"

"Sounds good?" I rose from the couch, squeezing between the table and her knees. I felt a strange, compelling urge to make Frances' birthday one to remember. I knew it wasn't my job to take care of her but I just wanted to do something to ease her sadness.

As I passed, Frances caught my wrist. "Thank you again for the poster, and thank your parents for the gin. I really appreciate it, okay?"

Her sincerity made my heart swell. "You're very welcome."

She held my hand for a little longer, her thumb caressing the back of it. A moment passed before she realised what she was doing and she quickly let go. A faint blush tinted her cheeks as I continued to the kitchen. What was that about? Could it be that Frances was into me?

Nah, she'd never have agreed to be my fake-girlfriend if she had real feelings. And she knew I wasn't into girls so it seemed unlikely. Maybe just an innocent crush that would pass as we got to know each other better.

I returned with coffee and we toasted to her birthday, ordering breakfast takeaway to celebrate. We chatted amicably, eventually cracking into the gin while we waited for her friends to arrive for the party. Some of them had been over a couple of times so I no longer felt like a third-wheel, plus Jenna was coming too. Well, half of Platypus was invited and from what I'd heard, they loved celebrating birthdays. Any excuse to party.

Within half an hour, the flat was packed with people and our counter filled with bottles and all sorts of gifts for Frances. Someone had connected their phone to our speakers and music was blasting through our living room, turning any open space into dancefloor. While sipping from my gin, I watched Frances greet more friends at the door. They embraced like they'd known each other their entire life, but it was just as likely they'd met a couple of weeks ago. College friendships were easy to form and their fleeting nature wasn't always a bad thing.

"Daniels!"

I looked up at the sound of my name and spotted Jenna appearing from behind a group of girls that really nailed that androgynous look. Not dissimilar in clothing style to my roommate, and with loose clothing that left everything to the imagination. Frances wore it best though.

I tore my gaze away and greeted my best friend with a big hug. "Jennaaaaa! Ah, I'm so glad to see you."

"Same." She jumped in excitement. "I've been living in a love bubble but I've missed your little face. Woah, it's packed in here."

"Frances has a lot of friends. Come in, let me get you a drink. Oh, we're putting coats in your old room so you can have a look." I waved her along, clicking on the light so she could have a quick nosey around. I felt a little sneaky but Frances did say she was using her room as the vestiaire.

Jenna hummed appreciatively as she looked around the room. "Interesting. Okay, okay. Not bad. She's got her bed in a different place and aww, a fish tank."

"It's actually a coral tank," I supplied, putting her coat on the pile of jackets.

"No fish? That's kind of boring."

"I think it's cute. She's doing her dissertation on coral." I giggled. "That's a funny word. Dissertation. Disssssertation."

"How much have you drunk already?"

I shrugged. "Some. I don't know. We started after breakfast."

"Ah, the good old daytime drinking." She gave me a playful nudge as we made our way back to the living room. "Gosh, so many people."

"I know." I giggled and hiccuped as I opened the fridge. The floor was a little wobbly so I gripped the counter, steadying myself. "Want a drink?"

"Of course. I'll have whatever you're drinking cause it's clearly working."

SIXTEEN

Frances

THE PARTY WAS in full swing before it was even eight. I was surprised by how many people had shown up, despite the heavy rain and stormy weather, but I also knew it had nothing to do with me. Platypeople just loved partying. Between the music and the singing people, conversation wasn't really high on anyone's list but I didn't mind. It was fun just to have so many people over. Even some of the invited neighbours had come in to say hello and have a drink.

"I need the loo," Erin declared as she finished her drink. She kissed her girlfriend and waved at me. "I'll be right back."

The moment she was gone, Tash pulled me to the side. "I need to tell you something."

"I'm all ears."

My best friend shot me the widest grin. "I'm going to propose."

"Tash! Oh my god, that's amazing. When? How? Where?"

"I don't know yet. I think Erin is filming another Project soon so I want ask her when she's interviewing me." She checked over her shoulder and continued whispering. "Do you think that's a good idea?"

"I think it's a lovely idea. Aaaah, I can't believe you're getting married. You did it. You found the one." Even though I was ecstatic for her, the smallest pang of envy shot through me. My best friend was getting married and I had no one.

"Shh, shh, she's coming back. Act normal," Tash hushed as she turned around to her girlfriend like nothing happened.

While the two of them were happily chatting in their lovey dovey way, I glanced at the kitchen where Ivy was pouring her best friend a drink. Jenna said something that made her laugh and more jealousy passed through me. I knew it wasn't justified but it was hard not to feel a little territorial.

After all, I was the new roommate. I'd taken Jenna's place.

I finished my drink with a big swig, suppressing the urge to cough. "I'm just getting another."

My friends made a non-committal noise as I made my way over to the kitchen, joining Ivy and Jenna. "Hey, hey."

Once Ivy noticed me, she stumbled towards me, her cheeks rosy from the alcohol. "Francesss. Are you having fun at your party?"

"Yes, I sure am. Thanks for letting me throw it here."

She snaked her arm around my waist, leaning into me. "Of course. It's your birthday, isn't it?"

"Yes, it is." I swung my arm around her shoulders, trying to avoid Jenna's inquiring looks. I knew she was trying to figure out if there was something going on between us and maybe it was wrong of me, but I wasn't opposed to her assuming so. Even if it was only until Ivy set her straight.

Jenna shot me a polite smile. "So how are you liking my old room?"

"It's nice, I love the skylight," I replied tersely. I turned to look at Ivy, pulling her closer. "But the best part is my awesome roommate."

Ivy managed a smile before she broke away. "I need the bathroom!"

Left alone with Jenna, an awkward tension settled onto us. I'd never not got along with her but she seemed a lot more hostile ever since I moved in with here. Maybe she had a secret crush on Ivy.

No, she'd never have moved out if that was the case.

To bridge the silence, I reached in the upper cupboard for the bottle of gin. I'd deliberately put it out of reach so the others wouldn't drink my gift from Ivy's parents. I poured myself a good glug and put the bottle back behind some boxes of stale tea.

"Isn't that Ivy's gin?" Jenna asked, her tone sharp. "She always drinks that brand."

"No, her parents sent it to me for my birthday. I must've made a good impression last week." I took a big sip, savouring the bitter taste.

"You met them?"

"Yes, I tagged along for lunch. She kind of asked me to pretend to be her girlfriend to stop them from obsessing over her love life. Didn't Ivy tell you about this?"

The other girl shook her head slowly. "No, she conveniently didn't mention that... So you met Martha and Walt."

"I did. They seem nice."

"They are but their relationship with Ivy is complicated. I've known them almost my entire life so take my word for it."

I didn't know why, but it felt more like a threat than a good-natured warning. Not wanting to piss off Ivy's best friend, I held my hands up. "Don't worry, Ivy calls the shots."

"She better. I know we all love chasing a straight girl but Ivy isn't like that. You're wasting your time if you think you can turn her."

"I'm not trying to turn her."

"If you say so."

"I'm not," I repeated, the tension in the conversation palpable. I knew my reputation wasn't the best, but this was a little unnecessary. I'd never do anything to hurt Ivy. Besides, there was nothing going on so it didn't matter what she thought.

Before she could make another comment, my phone vibrated in my pocket. I pulled the device out, checking the caller ID. "It's my Mum, I got to take this."

With the loud music pounding through the flat, I stepped out onto the landing where it was a little quieter and with the door closed behind me, I answered the call. "Hello?"

"Frances! Happy birthday, sweetheart," Mum's voice trumpeted through the speaker.

A smile bubbled up in me. They remembered. "Thanks. How's Dad?"

"Loving the sun. You know, he's really getting that tan going. He looked a bit ridiculous in the beginning, some would say alarmingly red, but he's all sexy now."

"Gross. So you're enjoying your trip?"

"We are. Did you buy something nice with your birthday money?"

"Not yet." I leaned against the window sill, watching the trickling rain on the glass. "But I'm thinking I might get a new coral or something."

"You should. You always loved those things, ever since you were small."

"They're not things, Mum. They're animals."

"Right, right, of course. Hey, listen. Your dad and I have something to tell you. We met a lovely couple yesterday and they have this wonderful place in the Bahamas. They offered it to us at a great price so we'll be celebrating the holidays at the beach. Isn't that amazing?"

My great mood immediately dissipated and a heavy weight sank to the bottom of my stomach. "So you're not going to be back for Christmas?"

"No, we won't be reachable but I called your aunt and she said you're more than welcome to join for the festivities and celebrate Christmas with your nieces and nephews. Now I know they're vegetarian but she said they'd make a chicken especially for you." Mum sang, sounding cheery as ever. "We've put some more money in your bank account, that should hold you over. Make sure to buy yourself something nice, okay?"

"Wow, great." The bitter taste in my mouth made it hard to sound happy but Mum was oblivious to it, like always.

"Anyway, I've got to go. We've got a game of pool going on with our cabin neighbours. Enjoy the rest of your birthday and we'll see you in the new year! Eeeh, exciting."

"Yeah, see you," I muttered in the speaker, quickly hitting the red button. I should be used to this by now but it still stung. More than that, it hurt that they were gone over my birthday but Christmas was worse.

I stared at the phone in my hands, trying not to kick something or throw it down the stairs. Why did they even have me if they didn't like having children?

The door shrieked open and a blast of music came out of the flat as Ivy swayed out, her flowery dress moving along with her hips. "Hey, there you are."

I shot her a half-hearted smile. "Sorry, just needed some air."

"You sure?" She reached up and wandered her

fingers over my face, tickling my forehead. "What's with all the wrinkles?"

"It's not important."

She propped herself up on the window sill too, a little unsteady on her feet. She giggled tipsily as she turned her attention to me. "I know your thunder look. What's the matter?"

I sighed. "Just got off the phone with my mum. They're not going to be back in time for Christmas."

"Aww." Ivy put her hand on my leg, her touch reassuring. "I'm sorry."

"It's okay. They always do stuff like this. They were out of the country for my high school graduation and I celebrated my eleventh birthday with the neighbours. Not the saddest birthday I've had. Got a slice of chocolate cake out of it, so. You know, that's birthday-like."

Unexpectedly, Ivy pulled me into a hug. Her breath was warm on my skin and her arms tight and comforting. She smelled like a summer meadow and roses, her perfume floral and intoxicating. We hadn't had much physical contact since the kiss mishap and I felt myself melt into her embrace, holding on to her.

Maybe it was off the back of the incident and everyone's insinuations but it felt like a different kind of hug than usual. It was longer, intimate, like it meant something more perhaps.

Ivy released a soft burp and giggled. "Sorrrry."

Or it just meant that she was way past tipsy.

I pulled back, dismissing my thoughts. "I think you've had too much to drink."

"Nahhh, I've only had a little bit," she slurred, showing me the tiniest gap between her thumb and index finger. "Hey, I know. You should go with me to my parents for the holidays!"

A first smile tugged on my lips. I appreciated the invitation but I knew she didn't mean it. Besides, even if she did, I wouldn't want to intrude. I wasn't going to ruin her family Christmas just because I couldn't have one.

Affectionately, I patted her head. "Let's get you some water."

She looked at me with the most horrified expression. "Water? It's a party. I want tequilaaaaa."

I chucked. "We do have lemons and salt."

She jumped off the window sill, whooping as she ran back into the flat. "Shots, shots, shots!"

Everyone cheered and with a bemused smile, I followed her in, ready to drink the night away. After all, it was my birthday and even if my parents didn't care, plenty of people in the room did. That was good enough.

SEVENTEEN

Ivy

I OPENED MY EYES, frozen in the cold wet linens. Oh no. Oh no, no, no. Why was my bed wet? Did I drink so much I had an accident?

Scared to move, I slowly raised my head so I could peek at the sheets. A large, wet stain on the duvet alarmed me but it was situated around my chest, not in the downstairs area.

A tentative sniff confirmed it too. Not pee.

Oof. I plopped back down, only to realise this didn't explain the situation. I jolted back up and a large droplet hit my forehead, splattering down my nose. I looked up, my eyes widening in worry. The darkened ceiling hung over me as a bad omen.

I quickly got out of bed, making my spinning headache even worse. My bare feet hit a puddle and my toes squelched on the floor. "Oh my god! Why is everything wet!?"

Shivering and shaking, I tip-toed out of my room and knocked on Frances' door. It was only when I heard stumbling that I realised I could be barging in on something. Not important enough, the roof was leaking.

The door opened to a crack and Frances stuck her head out, her hair standing up in all directions. "Yes?"

"The ceiling is leaking." I picked at my wet shirt. "I'm soaked. It's dripping right onto my bed."

She yawned as she stumbled out in nothing more than a loose tank top and some boxer shorts. She scratched her messy head, her sleepy confusion adorable. "What?"

"It's raining. I think our roof is damaged." I turned too fast and my pinching headache made the world spin. The sudden urge to vomit hit me and I pressed my hands against my mouth to hold it back.

"You okay?" Frances asked.

I swallowed the bile back and nodded. "Hmm-hmm. Come look at my room."

My roommate joined me in the doorframe and gasped. "Oh no, that's not good. Oh, it's all wet. How did you sleep through this?"

"I was really, really drunk," I explained.

"Ahh, I see. Gosh. What can we do about this?"

"I guess we should call the landlord." I looked up at the dripping ceiling. "And I guess I should move my stuff out of the way."

Frances nodded. "Yeah, totally. We should push everything into the living room, just to be sure."

"You don't have to help," I quickly said. I didn't want her to think that was why I woke her.

"Nonsense, of course I'll help. Here, let's put your blankets in the wash and hang your duvet up to dry. And we should prop your mattress up too so it doesn't get wet." She walked around the puddle so she could grab my pillow. "Oh, and put a towel or bucket under that."

"You're so practical," I complimented, grabbing my wet blankets and dragging them out, not caring whether they were on the floor or not. They were already wet anyway. I shoved them into the washing machine and continued pushing stuff out of my room, trying to ignore my throbbing headache. This was so not what I wanted to do after a long night of drinking and partying.

In hungover silence, Frances and I emptied my

room out. By the time we were done, the living room looked like a sardine can. The couch was pushed all the way back against the wall with my dresser next to the fridge and my mattress drying next to the radiator.

Tired, I collapsed on my kitchen chair. "Guess I'll have to call the landlord."

Frances nodded, looking equally as exhausted. "Yeah, good idea."

"I'm sorry I woke you, I panicked." I yawned as I grabbed my phone. "Why don't you go back to bed?"

"I might. Night, Ivy."

I was only a little jealous that she could return to bed. I searched for the landlord's number in my contact list and—

"Son of a bitch!" Frances shouted.

Concerned, I rushed over to her room, almost tripping over a box of my stuff. I gripped the doorframe and bumped right into Frances on her way out. "You okay? What's wrong?"

"The damn ceiling is leaking in my room too!" She pointed at the light fixture. "Look!"

"Oh my god, what's wrong with this bloody flat?" I forced back a burp and sighed. "Come on, let's move your stuff out too before it gets ruined."

"Uggh, I don't want to," Frances complained. "Can you help me move the tank?"

It took another hour to clear out her room and turn the living space and kitchen into a hoarder's dream. Squashed on the couch, between a box of clothes and a stack of old college books, I called the landlord's number. For good measure, I put it on speaker so Frances can hear from her pillow on the floor.

The line rings five times before someone answered. "Hello, this is Tom."

"Hi, Tom. It's Ivy. I'm calling with a bit of a situation." Nerves shot through me. Even though I knew it wasn't our fault that it was raining inside, I was worried the landlord would blame us and make us pay for it. I shot Frances a worried look, drawing some reassurance from her smile. With a big breath, I blurted out the issue. "There's quite a heavy storm and umm, well, the roof is leaking."

"Is it? Where's the leak?"

"Both the bedrooms. We've just moved everything out of the way and we've put buckets under them but we're worried there will be more leaks that'll ruin our stuff," I said, picking at a loose thread of my dress.

"I'll send one of my builders over to take a look. It'll be somewhere tomorrow or the day after," Tom answered, not sounding very panicked.

I gulped. "Okay... neither of us can use our bedrooms though..."

The line crackled with static. "I've got to run. I'll text you an update."

"But—" I growled when the call cut out and tossed my phone in one of the many piles of stuff. "Guess we're stuck here."

"Rude," Frances commented, gesturing to the mess. "Guess we're camping in the living room."

With a sigh, I put the pillow over my head. "Ugggh. Such a vague answer on the builder as well. This is so not fun."

She reached out to touch my knee. "It's going to be fine. We can book a hotel?"

"Yeah, I'm not flush enough for that," I admitted, already worrying about the expenses of the month. With the holidays and all the gift giving, my budget was spread thin already. "It'll be fine. I could always leave a little early to spend Christmas and New Year with my parents."

A strange look flashed through Frances' eyes but she quickly masked it with a smile. "Yeah, totally. If we stack everything better, we should have space to put our mattresses down. It'll be like a sleepover."

I smiled. "Sounds fun. I haven't had a sleepover since high school."

EIGHTEEN

Frances

THE BATHROOM DOOR opened and Ivy tiptoed out in her pink pyjamas, looking a little shy about the shortness of her bottoms. She jumped onto her side of the mattress, diving under the covers. "Did you change the bucket?"

I nodded, nestling under my duvet. "Yeah, I did it while you were changing."

"Thanks." She groaned. "Ugh, I forgot to turn the light off."

"I'll get it," I said, tossing the covers off and getting up. Even with the lights dimmed, it wasn't quite dark. The moonlight coming in through the large windows illuminated the living room enough that I caught Ivy staring at me.

Self-conscious, I pulled my tank top down and quickly got under the blankets again, even though it was hot in the room. The radiators blasting heat to dry everything were quickly turning the flat in a sauna.

I stared up at the ceiling, incredibly aware of how close Ivy was lying next to me. The lack of space meant we were sharing my queen sized mattress. While there was plenty of space, it felt incredibly intimate. I hoped she wasn't too uncomfortable…

"What a day, huh?" she voiced, ruffling the sheets. "I'm so glad I don't have work tomorrow."

"Yeah, I'm skipping class. I'll just work on my dissertation or something." I glanced at my tank which we'd put next to the door. The soft gurgling of the water and the pump's humming was a soothing, reassuring sound for me but maybe Ivy would find it disturbing.

"Do some of your coral glow in the dark?" she questioned, pushing herself up to look at them.

I smiled. "Not quite, but I'd love some glow in the dark ones."

"That would be fun," she commented, sitting up even more. "The yellow one looks like it's waving."

"Did I tell you I decided on names for them?"

She looked at me with excitement in her eyes. "No, you didn't! Tell me."

"Okay, so the blue one is Gary. Then the pink, spiky one is Pinky. And the yellow one with the waving hands is The Astronomer. That's my favourite."

"The Astronomer," she echoed. "What a fancy name. I like it."

"Yeah, your comment about them needing names hit home. I don't know why they didn't have any, I used to name everything when I was little. That's what you get for being an only child. I was always a bit lonely." I turned on my side so I could face the other woman. "I guess that's what I always loved about coral. People overlook them but there's so much more to them that meets the eye. They're reliable and useful, they're home to so many types of fish. They're always exactly where you left them too, just swaying in the water, being their dependable self."

Ivy sat up, crossing her legs. "Sounds like maybe you related to them?"

"Yeah, I did." I gulped. "That's a little pathetic, isn't it?"

"Not at all. It's hard being lonely." She wrapped her arms around her shins and rested her head on top of her knees. "When I was sixteen, my brother really clashed with my parents. They kind of kicked him out slash he just never returned from college. We used to be really close growing up and suddenly, he was just kind of… gone. It was really hard."

I decided against reaching out. The set-up was already so intimate and personal, I didn't want to cross any lines. Instead, I got up and made my way to the kitchen. "I think we should have some ice cream. What do you think?"

Ivy's relieved face said it all. She nodded eagerly. "God, yes. Now you're speaking my language."

I returned with two cold bowls and little spoons. The wintery weather didn't usually call for ice cream but the heat inside and the emotional unloading demanded it. We clinked our bowls together and dug in, enjoying having something to do.

Between bites, I leaned back against the couch which was doubling as a makeshift headboard. "I'm glad you like the coral though. My ex absolutely hated them. I'm pretty sure she killed the last ones."

Ivy gasped. "That's awful. I hoped you dumped her after that."

"I dumped her before it, she made duplicates of my house key. And she's not even the worst person I've dated."

"Now you've got me intrigued."

I finished my ice cream and put the bowl away. I

wasn't sure if it was the intimate setting or the nightly time, but it felt like Ivy and I were reaching a new level of friendship. I was happy to share and bond. "I once dated a pathological liar."

She gasped as she shuffled closer, leaning against the front of the couch. "Tell me more. No, tell me everything."

I chuckled. "Okay, well... Her name was Olga and it was one of those instant spark things. When we met, we just clicked. We had so much in common. She moved to the city a couple of months ago to get away from her homophobic family and start fresh. I thought that was really brave."

She nodded, finishing her ice cream. "Totally."

"Yeah. We met in Rainbow Central and danced the night away. Did other things to pass the night too. It was just one of those natural things. She was a teacher, had an adorable ginger cat that I loved. We took vegan cooking classes together because she didn't eat meat. That's where I learned to make my favourite pasta sauce, and we found all the places in the city that you could see the stars from. It was magical."

"So what happened?"

A slight pause hung between us as I recalled the heartbreak. "One day, we were out shopping and we ran into this other woman. She was seething. Turns out, it was her wife."

"Oh no." She gasped. "Oh, that's not what you want."

"No, not at all. Olga tried to deny everything but when it didn't work, she jumped in a taxi and rode away. I went for drinks with her wife, turns out she was never a teacher. She worked for her family, who was lovely and accepting of their marriage."

"Ouch."

"Yeah. They'd been together for years and Olga often went on business trips, pretending to be someone totally different apparently. Oh, and her name wasn't Olga, it was Adelaide or whatever. And she wasn't vegan either. I ate tofu for three months for her," I muttered bitterly.

"That bitch." She touched my arm, too invested. "What about the cat?"

"A friend's. She was cat-sitting."

"Wow. And I thought my last boyfriend dumping me for his childhood crush was rough. I know it doesn't sound bad but she was also, technically, his step-sister."

"Ooooof. You're right, that's bad." I nestled against the couch and released a dramatic sigh. "Why are relationships this hard?"

"I don't know. I always thought, hoped, that if I

met the right person, it would just be effortless. That we'd be friends, know everything about each other."

"No secrets, no lies," I added. "A real team."

"Exactly. I'm starting to think it doesn't exist."

"Maybe not." I glanced at her, the question burning on the tip of my tongue. "You never thought about getting together with Jenna?"

"With Jenna?" Ivy chuckled. "No, gosh. We're so not compatible."

"Cause she's a woman?" I asked, eyeing her up for her reaction.

"No, cause she's a handful. She's like a cat. Comes home late at night, no explanation where she's been. Only wants affection on her terms. Oh, and gives crappy gifts. Once, she got me a stapler."

"That can be useful," I commented slowly. Her answer didn't make it sound like she was completely against dating a girl, but I was probably reading into things.

With a chuckle, Ivy adjusted her pillow. "I already had one. Plus, she stole this one from her professor. I don't know why, she just said it had my name on it. Not even the worst of all her presents."

I didn't know why but her delivery made me laugh. "I don't know her that well but I believe you."

"Yeah, her girlfriend is a saint for putting up with

her. I love Jenna to death but man, she can be a pest. Can you believe she's studying to be a teacher?"

"I… can, actually."

We lapsed into a comfortable silence, listening to the sound of the rain on the roof. It would've been more soothing and enjoyable if we didn't know it was pouring through the roof too. The dripping coming from our rooms and the continuous emptying of the buckets didn't really elicit a cosy feel.

Ivy released a sigh as she stared up at the drying towels and sheets. "This reminds me of when I used to build forts with Steven. We'd always come up with ridiculous rules and passwords to keep our parents out. I wonder if that's how people feel in their VIP clubs."

"Totally." I looked up at the ceiling, taking in the raggedy sight of all our belongings drying. "I never built a fort."

"No. Never?"

"Never."

Ivy threw her covers off and bounced up to move a couple of boxes. "Well, this can count as your first fort then. I'm just going to move this towel and push this lamp over here and tadaa. It's a fort! Now we just need a password."

Infected by her playfulness, I moved some of the pillows to form a wall. "It's a weird fort."

"We're weird."

I chuckled. "So what should the password be?"

"Well, we often picked our favourite foods or a tv character from a show we were watching."

"The password can be ice cream."

"Or pasta."

"Or gin," I giggled.

"There we go! Now that's a password I can get behind." Ivy jumped back on the bed, a lot less self-conscious than before. Looked like the sharing had made us more comfortable in each other's presence. At least that was something.

Not able to stop myself, I glanced at the other girl and a warmth welled up in me. I really enjoyed spending time with her and she was easy on the eyes too. When my gaze lingered on her curves and my ears heated up, I knew I was in trouble.

I quickly flopped down on the bed, diverting my attention to the ceiling. Why was I always like this? I couldn't make a friend without developing a crush. If she knew the way I was looking at her, surely she'd be disgusted or feel violated.

Ivy's sheets rustled. "You okay?"

"Yeah, just suddenly feel tired." I yawned

demonstratively, hoping the dark hid my blushing cheeks. "I think I'm ready to sleep."

"Night, Frances."

My stomach fluttered slightly at the way she said my name and I pulled my sheets up to my nose. "Goodnight."

NINETEEN

Ivy

I CURLED TIGHTER into the warm body next to me, the smell of cinnamon warm and inviting. In my sleepy haze, it took another moment or two to realise something wasn't adding up.

Disoriented, my eyes fluttered open and I pulled back just enough to identify the person I was cuddling with. Somewhere in our sleep, I'd rolled over on Frances' side and become her big spoon. Pressed tightly against her back and with both arms around her, we were snuggling in an intimate embrace, more intimate than friends usually slept.

A little embarrassed, I pulled away and rolled

back over to my side of the bed. The cold mattress confirmed I'd probably been snugging her most of the night and I immediately missed her warmth. There was a slight temptation to roll back and cuddle into my roommate but that wasn't very fair. Instead, I took in the chaotic living room by daylight and enjoyed the feeling of a lazy morning. I desired a good cup of coffee but that would wake Frances so I played games on my phone until the woman next to me stirred.

She smacked her mouth sleepily as she sat up, her short hair sticking up like a bird's nest. She looked adorable and a wave of affection washed over me when I looked at her.

"Morning," I chimed, trying to ignore the stirring in my chest.

Frances yawned. "Morning. Well, looks like we survived our first night in the fort."

"We did. How did you sleep?"

She rotated her head. "Not too bad, actually. I feel well rested. Did we…" She shot me an intense, curious look. "Never mind. Coffee?"

I nodded, curious to her unspoken question but I could tell from her flighty demeanour that she wasn't going to elaborate. She jumped out of the bed, stretching as she made her way to the kitchen. I couldn't help myself from watching her go, admiring her toned legs and arms. She walked with a certain casual flair that really added to her boyish charm. Yet I could tell there was some curvature hiding under her loose tank tops.

Why was I thinking like this? My cheeks heated up as I shook my thoughts away. Things were great between us at the moment, I didn't want to ruin that.

The coffee machine gurgled as Frances got it started and it didn't take long for the smell to fill the flat. I made my way to the kitchen and pulled two of our chairs out from the mess. If someone came into our home, they'd probably think we were hoarders.

I put the chairs on the stone kitchen floor, our table stuck under a bunch of boxes and crap from my room. "Guess we're eating breakfast on our lap."

"Or in bed?" Frances suggested, turning around with two steaming mugs of coffee.

"Sounds fun," I blurted out eagerly. I followed her back to the mattress, sitting closer to her than necessary. Our fingers touched when she handed me the mug and a little shiver ran down my back. Oh man, what had gotten into me?

I quickly took a sip of coffee to hide my reaction, hoping she hadn't noticed. From the looks of it, she hadn't, which made sense. Why would she be looking at me like that, she knew I wasn't into women. That being said…

No, I couldn't think like that. I'd heard Jenna complain about bicurious and experimenters enough to know I couldn't be like that. I was probably just confusing our growing friendship for something else.

"Did you check the buckets?" Frances questioned, nudging to the bedrooms.

"Not yet. Do we dare?"

"We dare."

Giggling, we crossed the room to check the potential damage. My door creaked open to reveal a bucket near overflowing. The towels on the floor were dark and wet, dirty from whatever roof dirt it was bringing in.

"God, this is a mess. I hope the landlord gets this fixed quickly." My phone vibrated and I quickly pulled it out, hoping it was the landlord. "Speaking off… Nope, it's my mum. Sorry, I got to take this."

"Tell her thank you for the gin," Frances quipped as she made it back to the living room.

"I will!" I called after her, propping myself up on the window sill for lack of seating options. "Hey, Mum."

"Lemon drop, I heard there's a storm near you. Is it bad?"

"It's alright. Although our roof is leaking. But don't worry, the landlord is sending a builder over."

"Aww, that's annoying. Make sure he fixes it quickly, okay? That's his responsibility."

"I know, I know."

"Good. So have you decided on when you're coming over for the holidays yet? We're hosting a little neighbourly event with the Walkers and we want to make sure you're here for it."

"Umm... I don't know yet. I was thinking right before Christmas but if this leak keeps up, maybe sooner. The print shop doesn't need me over the holidays anyway."

"Marvellous. I'll make up the guest room for you two."

"Two? What—" I caught a glimpse of Frances passing by the door and quickly caught on. "Oh, no, no, Frances isn't—"

"You're not splitting up for the holidays, are you? You have to spend those together! Now that you've finally found someone. Bring her. We loved her, she's such a nice girl."

"I'll ask," I responded hesitantly. No longer able to sit still, I paced back and forth on the dry patches of wood. "But no guarantees. She might have other plans."

Although if I remembered correctly, her parents were on a cruise or something. I recalled her telling me during her party but the drunken haze made it hard to remember. I'd have to ask her but obviously not while I was on the phone with Mum.

"Your dad and I look forward to seeing you again. He said he'll make your favourite apple pie. Oh, and your brother is coming too."

"Steven is coming for Christmas?"

"Yes! It's a time for family, isn't it?"

I refrained from commenting on it or the five last Stevenless Christmases. But knowing my big brother was going to be there was exciting. I missed him so it would be nice to see him again.

"I'll let you know when I'm coming, okay?" I glared at the leaking ceiling, not pleased with the situation. "And I'll ask Frances if she wants to come. Oh, she said thank you for the gin. It was really thoughtful to send it."

"It was no problem. See you soon!"

The line disconnected and I returned to the living room where Frances was chilling on the small space of free couch. The TV on the other side of the room was on and playing her flower show.

When she noticed me, she pressed pause and smiled. "Everything okay?"

"Yeah, just my mum wanted to know when I'm coming over for the holidays." I leaned against one of the boxes. "Do I remember correctly that your parents aren't going to be back to celebrate with you?"

Frances' souring expression gave me my answer. "Yeah... They're off on another one of their cruises."

"So you're not doing anything for Christmas?"

"Well... I'm invited to go to my aunt but they're all vegetarian. Nut roast isn't very festive to me. She did offer to make a chicken for me but it's always so dry."

"Okay, right. Well, so... hear me out. Why don't you come with me? Mum pulls out all the stops when cooking dinner, there's a Christmas tree, Christmas market in the village, it's a lot of fun."

Frances shot me a surprised look. "You... want me to come with you?"

"Yes. Mum asked whether you were coming. I know pretending to be my girlfriend isn't exactly festive but I promise it'll be fun. And you can't possibly spend the holidays here," I said, gesturing around the cramped flat. "I got a text from the landlord. He's sending builders over tomorrow but it'll take a couple of days before it'll be fixed."

My roommate wasn't convinced. "But you'd have to lie to your family the whole time."

"It won't be that hard. They have no clue about lesbian relationship. They used to ask if Jenna and I were together. You'd be doing me a huge favour cause I really don't want them to nag me all week why my girlfriend didn't come along."

"If you're sure I'm not imposing…"

"No, not at all," I answered, maybe a little too quickly, or eagerly. The idea of playing Frances' girlfriend made my chest tighten and I wanted it for slightly different reasons than last time. Was that bad? Probably.

Frances thought for a moment and then nodded. "Sure, why not. I've got nothing else on and it beats staying in our leaky flat or my aunt's nut roast."

Yes! I could just jump for joy.

TWENTY

Frances

FIVE DAYS at Ivy's parents, pretending to be her girlfriend. It seemed like a good idea until we were pulling up on their driveway and the reality of it all set in. I was really going to spend five days lying to her parents, and to a degree, her. Maybe I should've told her about my little crush but what good would that do? I knew she wouldn't reciprocate my feelings and I wasn't going to do anything to make her uncomfortable so... Why couldn't I enjoy the holidays with a family that cared instead of having to be on my own?

I stalled the car, drawing in a deep breath. "Ready?"

Ivy unclicked her seatbelt as she climbed out of the passenger's seat. "Nope. But let's do it anyway."

A chuckle bubbled up in me. "We don't have to lie. We can just say we've broken up but decided to stay friends. That's very common for lesbians."

She snorted as we made our way through the front yard. "No, then they'll pester us the entire week to get us back together." She paused and reached out to take my hand. "But if you're uncomfortable pretending, we don't have to."

I stared at our joined hands, intertwining our fingers. I knew I was being selfish for saying yes but at least it was helping her out. "I'm up for it."

"Thanks. I owe you." She tugged me along, a renewed bounce in her step.

More guilt laced through me but I pushed it away and instead, conjured a smile as we entered her parents' house. Just like last time, her mum was pottering around the kitchen until she saw us.

"Hello, darlings." She turned her stove off and greeted us at the door, hugging Ivy tightly. "Have you lost weight?"

Ivy smiled. "I don't think so."

"Well, you look a little thinner," her mum

decided. She released her daughter and turned to me, pulling me in a hug too. "Frances! So glad you could make it."

"Thanks for inviting me."

"Of course. We want to get to know Ivy's partner. You know, I'm not surprised she ended up with a girl. She never liked the boys much, not even in kindergarten. She always said she was going to marry her doll." Martha chuckled as she waved us in. "What do you both want to drink?"

"Just some water," Ivy answered, turning to me. "I'll take your coat."

Maybe I was imagining it, but there was a difference to her tone, in the way she was looking at me. She was really taking this fake-girlfriend thing seriously and part of me loved it.

"Thanks, babe." The moment I said it, I regretted my choice of pet name. I could do better than that.

Ivy's blushing smile made up for it though and made me want to try out other cute things to call her.

While she got us a drink, it gave me a chance to chat to her mum.

"So are you and Ivy celebrating the holidays with your side of the family too?" Martha inquired.

I shook my head. "No, they're on a cruise so they won't be back until the new year."

"Oh. So you're not seeing them at all?"

"No. We're not very close," I admitted.

"Aww, darling." Martha patted my shoulder. "Well, don't you worry. You're part of the family now so we'll take good care of you."

I felt myself get a little misty-eyed. "Thank you, that's really sweet."

Ivy returned with two glasses of water, immediately picking up on my teary state. She cast her concerned gaze on me. "You okay?"

I conjured a smile but I wasn't sure I was convincing her. She was too perceptive for that. "I'm great."

"Okay… Let's get out of Mum's hair.." She waved me along to their living room.

Just like last time, her father was sitting in his armchair, a newspaper on his lap and the tv playing in the background. He looked up and his face brightened when he saw Ivy.

I wondered if my face did the same when Ivy walked into the room. Probably…

"Ivy. Come give your old man a hug."

Like last time, I lingered behind them as they embraced. It was strange to see an affectionate family that hugged and kissed, instead of my Mum and Dad's disinterested attitudes. I always thought

157

I'd been missing out but seeing Ivy and her parents, it really drove home how different things.

"You remember Frances, my girlfriend," Ivy introduced, her fingers brushing down my arm.

A little shiver ran down my spine from the way she touched me. I had to admit, I liked being called her girlfriend.

Ivy's dad nodded from his chair. "Nice to see you again."

"Thanks for having me. Oh, and thank you for my birthday gift. That was really lovely," I told him sincerely.

Walter smiled gruffly. "Don't you worry about that." He grunted as he got up from his chair. "You two wait here, I've got something for you."

I glanced at Ivy, who shrugged and seemed just as surprised. We sat down on the leather couch, the cushions dipping and pushing us closer together. Not that I minded. If anything, playing Ivy's girlfriend was giving me a taste of the real thing and made me want more.

"You okay?" she asked, her concern touching.

"I'm alright," I answered, briefly touching her knee. I kept a close eye on her reaction, wanting to be sure I wasn't making her uncomfortable. It didn't seem so. If anything, Ivy leaned into me, giving me the confidence to repeat the gesture, this time lingering a little longer.

The door opened and I jolted up, feeling guilty that I'd been caught making a move on Ivy, before realising there was no reason I had to do that.

Walt chuckled. "You don't have to pretend for my sake. I know what you youngsters get up to. You don't want to know how many times I caught Steven making out with a girl. Little bugger was always too charming for his own good."

Ivy and I exchanged a bemused look, the irony not escaping us. I trailed my hand down her back, a light touch just for the sake of touching.

"Anyway, this is for you." Walt handed Ivy a brown envelope.

She stared at it, confused. "What's this?"

"An envelope. You have to open it," he teased.

Ivy rolled his eyes at his lame joke as she ripped into the envelope. She gasped, her eyes widening. "Dinner for two… at Le Chateau? Are you serious?"

"I know what it's like to be young and in love. You don't want to be cooped up all day with us old people. You should go out, have a nice date just the two of you. It's all paid for so you don't have to worry about a thing."

"Daddd. That's so sweet, thank you." Ivy bounced up so she could give him a tight hug.

Not sure what to do, I smiled. "Thank you, that's

a real treat." I had to admit, the prospect of going to a fancy restaurant and having a date with Ivy was getting me really excited. Who knew what could happen…

It was the season of miracles.

TWENTY-ONE

Ivy

EVEN THOUGH I knew it wasn't a real date, I still felt nervous. I felt more nervous than I had in a long while. Not just because I wanted to make sure my parents didn't find out about our arrangement, but because this was an opportunity to get to know Frances better. Maybe the romantic setting and nice food would even spark something between us?

I still wasn't quite sure if I wanted that but the idea was quickly growing more and more tempting.

Nervously, I smoothed my dress down and with a last glance in the bathroom mirror, I made my way back to the guest room. I softly knocked on the door, not just wanting to barge in.

"Come in," Frances shouted.

I pushed inside, hoping I wasn't overdressed. Any worry fell away when I saw Frances in her suit. The stiff fabric clung to her body in all the right ways and really highlighted how tall she was. She'd combed her unruly hair back neatly and was even wearing some lip gloss.

"Wow," I muttered, doing a double and triple take. "You look fantastic."

"Yeah?" She plucked some dust from her jacket. "You think so?"

"I knew you'd look good in a suit," I replied, recalling an earlier conversation.

Her smile grew and she looked even more beautiful. "Thank you. You don't look so bad yourself either. Damn. I'm lucky."

"Lucky?"

She nodded, stepping into my personal space. My breath hitched when she leaned in. Was she going to kiss me? Just the thought had me parting my lips.

But instead of a kiss, she brought her lips to my ear. "I'm lucky that I get to take you out on a date. I know it's pretend but I'll take it."

A shiver ran through me as her hot breath tickled the shell of my ear. She smelled like cinnamon and anise, which I never cared much for but it was lovely on her. Intoxicating.

"You're cute when you blush," she teased when she stepped back. "Shall we?"

A little dazed, I nodded. "Ready."

"Shall I drive?"

"No, we can walk into town. If that's okay."

With her hands in her pockets, she nodded. "Sure, are you going to be okay with your heels?"

"I've got flats in my bag," I replied, touched by her concern. She was so thoughtful, it put all my exes to shame.

We chatted and laughed all the way to the restaurant, which was a lot posher than expected. I'd passed by it many times on my way to school but never been so this was exciting. The dazzling lights and the classical music were a lot more sophisticated than I was used to and nervous and feeling out of place, I gave the waitress my last name, half-expecting her to turn us away for not fitting in. She didn't seem fazed in the slightest and waved us along, showing us to a table in the corner. With a flickering candle and dimmed lights, it was a really intimate and romantic setting.

"Wow, it's so cosy here," Frances commented as she sat down opposite of me.

"This is the fanciest place I've ever been in," I

said, smoothing out the linen tablecloth. "They have fabric napkins!"

The other girl smiled. "When I was little, we were always going to places like this. Rich parents."

"Ooh, right.. I forgot." A slight awkwardness hung between us from the mention and I wasn't sure whether this was something to talk about on a date. Then again, I wanted her to be able to talk to me. "Are you upset that you're not celebrating with your family?"

Frances fiddled with the menu. "A little, if I'm honest. But that's on me for thinking they'd be better this year. I should thank you."

Surprised, I adjusted my chair. "Why?"

"For inviting me along and insisting. Otherwise, I would've spent Christmas alone or drunk in Rainbow Central. Instead, I get to spend it with you and your family. I feel blessed, even if it's pretend."

Hearing her say that made my heart overflow. I reached across the table, gingerly touching her hand. "The girlfriend thing is a little fib to get my parents off my back but it's not all pretend. Our friendship is real. You can come along every year, whether we're in a 'relationship' or not."

Frances intertwined our fingers, a soft, grateful look passing through her eyes. "Ivy…"

There was a strange intensity in the way she said

my name and I leaned forward, eager to hear what she had to say.

"Can I get you started on a drink?" a waitress asked, stopping by our table and breaking the tension.

I pulled back, our hands breaking apart. "Um, yes. I'll have a kirr royal. Frances?"

"Is the komucha homemade?" she questioned, gesturing to the drink list.

"It is and really excellent," the waitress replied, all her attention directed to the other girl.

"I'll have that." Frances folded her menu up. "Can we order as well? Yeah? I think we're both doing menu A, isn't that right?"

"Yes, sounds great. Two menus A," I said, having mostly skim-read the menu and all the fancy words. I wanted the server to go away so we could continue our conversation. It sounded like Frances had something important to say.

With the server gone, the other girl smiled. "Oh, I love this song. I know a lot of people hate Christmas music but I just love the jingles."

"Huh? Oh yeah, it's great. Were you going to say something before?"

"Was I? I don't remember," she quipped nonchalantly. "Hey, did you say there's a Christmas market?"

"Yeah, there's one every year. It's small but it nails the atmosphere. Want to go after dinner?"

She smiled. "I'd love to."

"Great. Great, great, great." I cleared my throat, trying to dispel some of the awkward tension hanging between us. I didn't know why I was being so nervous, we'd shared plenty of meals. Although sitting in a fancy restaurant all dressed up was different. There was a constant feeling of being judged and I couldn't help but wonder what would happen if we ran into someone I knew.

Frances shot me a look. "Are you okay there? You seem a bit... I don't know, stressed?"

"Yeah, umm, a little. I don't go to these fancy places very often."

"Don't you worry, it's just like a regular restaurant," she reassured me.

The server arrived with our drinks and I took a sip from my kirr, trying to dispel some of the awkwardness. "I just feel like people are watching us," I whispered.

"Then we'll watch right back. Okay, see that couple in the corner. The older man with the white beard and the woman with the stuck-up smile? That looks like a mandatory anniversary date but he would rather be with his much younger mistress and she's secretly having an affair with his brother," Frances said, her eyes sparkling with mischief.

I chuckled. "You're literally just making that up."

"They're educated guesses. He keeps looking at the waitress' chest whenever she passes by and she's constantly on her phone. You try one."

"Okay…" I let my gaze travel around the dining room, my eye catching on a young couple near the window. The man in the suit finished his whisky and immediately ordered a new one. The woman's scowl didn't hide her displeasure but he didn't seem to notice, or care. "Over to the left, he has a drinking problem and she wants to go home."

"Evidently. Now make up the story," Frances encouraged.

Before I could elaborate, the waitress presented us with our appetisers. She put the large plates with small portions in front of us, not without shooting Frances a flirty smile. A twinge of jealousy shot through me but I held the green-eyed monster back, not wanting to ruin the evening with a spat.

I picked up my fork, not quite sure where to start. "I can't even remember what we got."

"It's broiled eel on a bed of wilted greens, with a sweet balsamic glaze, toasted pine nuts, and a celeriac chip," Frances read from the menu. "Huh, I don't think I properly registered that when we ordered. What a weird combo."

"A little," I admitted, pressing the side of my fork into the fish. It split apart in glistening flakes and a savoury aroma rose with the steam. "It smells good. Mmm, it tastes good too. I like that. That's like a thousand times better than anything I could cook."

"Delicious," Frances agreed. "Ooh, something just happened with your couple. Look, the woman just ordered a bottle of wine and I don't think he's very happy about it."

I glanced at the people by the window and chuckled. "If this was a cartoon, she'd have thunderclouds hanging above her head. I bet she passively-aggressively ordered the most expensive wine as a comment on his whisky habit."

"Yesss, that's good. Now he's saying he's not paying for that," Frances added between bites.

"Oh, look. Look, he's getting up to talk to the waiter. I bet he's cancelling the ring in the dessert."

Frances looked impressed. "Nice, so he was having some liquid courage for a proposal? I like it. Well done."

"This is a fun game," I admitted, finishing my fish. "I wonder what people would say about us. They're probably wondering what this clueless girl is doing in such a fancy restaurant."

"No, they're probably thinking that the guy looks a bit feminine and that he's punching above his weight glass with his beautiful date," Frances commented, gesturing to herself. "Then they'll realise I'm actually a girl and decide I'm *definitely* punching above my weight."

I blushed. "Oh, stop it. More like the other way around. I saw the waitress looking at you. Wherever we go, people stare at you and not in the judgy way. It's cause you're so cute."

The other girl raised one eyebrow, her smirk undeniable. "You think I'm cute?"

My cheeks got even hotter and I averted my gaze to a plant on the window sill. Luckily, the waitress arrived to pick up our empty plates, saving me from embarrassment. I needed to watch what I said or I was going to give Frances the wrong impression. Or considering I was indeed entertaining romantic thoughts, the right impression?

TWENTY-TWO

Frances

DINNER WAS a nice gesture from Ivy's parents but I could tell it wasn't our scene. Ivy was tense the entire way and what I hoped would be a romantic date turned out as something we had to wrestle through. I tried not to take it personally but I was a little deflated as we left the restaurant. If I hadn't agreed to the Christmas market earlier, I might've suggested we just go home. I wanted to get a good night's sleep before the long anticipated Christmas dinner.

"Oh, it's a lovely crisp night," Ivy commented as

we continued to the village. "I can already smell the waffles and spices. I hope they have mulled wine."

A smile tugged on my lips. Looked like it was the restaurant that put her on edge. She was more relaxed now, more back to her regular self. Some of the stress fell away and I took a deep breath, taking in the cold air. "It's lovely weather. Perfect for a date night."

Ivy hummed happily. "Agreed. But the date isn't over yet."

We continued on under the decorative lights, the enticing smells growing stronger. It wasn't long before the little wooden huts showed up on the square, complete with fairy lights and a large decorated Christmas tree. It wasn't too busy but there was a cosy atmosphere hanging between stalls. Just a bit of snow, and it would be picture perfect.

"Oooh, fresh pretzels!" Ivy exclaimed, reaching for my hand.

I chuckled, happily letting her pull me along. "Didn't we just have dinner?"

"Yeah, but the portions were miniature," she commented. She paused, her face scrunched up in her thinking way. "But you're right, we've already eaten."

I recognised that tone. Even though I was skinny, I'd been told it wasn't very ladylike to eat a lot. From some of Martha's comments, it wasn't hard to guess where Ivy's body insecurity came from either.

"Let's get a pretzel," I decided, pulling my wallet from my jacket. "Want to share so we can try as many different things?"

A hesitant look flickered through Ivy's eyes. "Are you sure?"

"Yes. You're right, the portions were small and it's a Christmas market! The fun is trying everything," I said, hoping to put her at ease. I didn't mind her curves, if anything, they made her look inviting and soft and irresistible. Much better than me with my chicken legs.

I bought a pretzel from the vendor and held it out to her, expecting her to take half. Instead, she leaned right in and took a big bite. I gasped dramatically and she giggled, her eyes sparkling with joy. A satisfied grin welled up in me, knowing I judged that right.

Happy to share, I took a bite from the soft pretzel too, enjoying the sweet flavour. Sharing food this way was basically a prelude to kissing.

We continued on, trying on some funny animal hats and warm scarves. At some point, Ivy looped her arm through mine and pressed herself into me. My chest fluttered from the closeness and I strutted around like a proud cock running the roost. I could see how people were looking at Ivy, I knew I brought the prettiest belle to the ball.

A stall with particularly aromatic mulled wine drew our attention. The spices smelled delightful and really put us into the holiday atmosphere.

"Shall we get some?" I proposed.

"We better," Ivy joked, handing some money to the vendor.

With a steaming paper cup in hand, we took place next to a barrel with a heater next to it. The smell of the nearby pine trees was nostalgic and the taste of the hot wine was delightful. I caught Ivy's gaze and she smiled at me. My stomach fluttered and despite myself, I was really starting to wonder if there was something more than friendship growing between us.

She caught me looking at her but didn't seem upset about it. If anything, her smile grew wider. Under different circumstances, maybe I'd have dared flirt a bit more but this was different. She'd told me plenty of times that she wasn't into women so it wasn't fair or smart to pursue her. If she was into me, she'd let me know.

I quickly took a sip from the mulled wine, letting the warm flavours mingle. "So—"

"Daniels?" A man paused next to our barrel. "Is that you?"

Ivy turned in his direction and gasped. "Timothy…? What are you doing here?"

"I'm in town to visit the parents. You?"

"Me too."

"Wow, what a coincidence. That's amazing. Come here you." He pulled her into a tight, familiar hug that got my stomach all in envious knots. I could make a pretty good guess on how they knew each other and I didn't like it one bit.

Ivy pulled away and took a step back. "So funny that I'm running into you here… Frances, this is Timothy. My ex…"

And there it was. The punch in the gut and slap in the face. A reminder that Ivy was not going to fall in love with me.

I gave a short, uninterested wave. "Hey."

Timothy smiled curtly before turning his attention back to Ivy. "So how've you been? What have you been up to?"

"Not much, to be honest. How are you and Cynthia?"

"We broke up." The guy pulled a sad face. "Yeah, things just didn't work out. I'm a free agent now. How long are you in town for?"

Ivy took a sip from her wine. "Not that long."

"Are you staying at your parents?"

She nodded. "We are."

Timothy completely ignored me. "Awesome. Hey, what are you doing for New Year's Eve? We should go out. Party at the Avant Garde, for old time's sake?"

"I don't think so," Ivy responded, her smile a little less sweet than before.

Her ex leaned on the barrel, pretty much excluding me from the conversation. "Why not?"

"You cheated on me… with your sister."

Timothy's ears burned red. "*Step*-sister. And we're no longer together."

I snorted loudly as the jealousy dissipated. It was good to put a name and face to the story. He gave me a dirty look but I no longer cared. Ivy might not fall in love with me but she certainly wasn't going to fall in love with this tosser.

"Well, tell her hi when you see her for family Christmas," Ivy commented sweetly. With a satisfied grin, she turned her back to him and aimed her charming smile at me. "I think I'm ready to go home. Shall we?"

"Music to my ears," I quipped, downing the last of my mulled wine. Grinning from ear to ear, I took a last look at Timothy's deflated face, wishing I could take a picture and frame it.

Ivy looped her arm through mine, pulling me

along. Her infectious laughter echoed into the night, the joy on her face worth everything.

She pressed herself into me, her warmth reaching all the way through. "This has been the best date ever."

I chuckled softly as we wandered through the cosy stalls. "Can I ask you something?"

"Of course."

"What's the difference between a real date and a friend date?" I dared, holding my breath. This was pretty much an admission of my feelings.

"Good question." Ivy thought about it for a moment. "Intent?"

I kept my gaze glued to the stones of the pavement. "Care to elaborate?"

"Well… A date is to see if you're romantically compatible and a friend date is to spend time with someone you like platonically?"

We paused underneath a large tree. "What if one party is trying to figure out if they're compatible but the other isn't?"

Ivy stared at me, looking pretty as a picture underneath the colourful tree. "I don't know. Why?"

I gulped, trying to ignore the urge to lean in and kiss her. With the fairy lights up in the branches and the soft music in the background, it felt like a perfect moment. Ivy's eyes shimmered and her soft lips looked so inviting and plump. Perfect for kissing. If she wasn't my roommate, maybe I'd have taken my shot but the prospect of awkward tension until one of us moved out was enough to knock some sense into me.

"Just making conversation," I responded, conjuring a smile. Instead of taking a step forward like I wanted, I took one back. The charged tension deflated and I could swear I saw some disappointment in Ivy's eyes. I was probably just seeing what I wanted to see.

Ivy smiled, but I could tell it wasn't genuine. "Ah… Yeah. You know, I'm actually pretty tired. Shall we call it a night? We've got Christmas tomorrow so we should get a good night's sleep"

I nodded reluctantly, silently cursing myself out for not taking the plunge. I was such an idiot.

TWENTY-THREE

Ivy

I WAS LOOKING FORWARD to Christmas day, even if things were slightly awkward with Frances after last night. I really thought she was going to kiss me but then... she hadn't. Maybe I was making things up, getting lost in the pretend. We were falling into a comfortable rhythm and light flirtations that were blurring the lines.

It was hard to sort out my confusing feelings when she was sitting next to me, one hand lightly resting on my leg. Her touch was light and unobtrusive but I could feel my thigh burning where she was touching me. If she moved her hand up higher—

Goodness, I shouldn't be thinking these kinds of things. Especially not in my parents' living room. How embarrassing.

Luckily, the doorbell went, giving me an excuse to get up. I jolted up, racing through the hallway and opening the front door. "Steven!"

"Hey, Yvi-Ivy." He stepped in, wrestling with his large coat and patting my head.

I playfully slapped his hand away. "I didn't realise you were coming too this year."

"Yeah, Mum insisted and I've got some news. Are they in?"

"Yup. Mum's in the kitchen and Dad in his chair."

He chuckled. "So nothing's changed then. Right, Dad first. Let's get this over with then."

I followed him into the living room, hoping everything would remain civil. It wouldn't be the first Christmas things blew up though, but maybe having Frances here would keep everyone on their best behaviour.

Dad barely looked up as we stepped into the salon. "Steven."

"Dad." My brother spotted Frances on the couch and raised a curious eyebrow. "Who's this?"

"This is Frances," I quickly introduced, reaching out to touch her shoulder. "My girlfriend."

"Girlfriend?" Steven stared at me, the cogs ticking in his head. "Really? Well, that explains some things."

"What?" Why did everyone act like me being gay made perfect sense?

He gave me a little shove. "Yeah, you were always marrying your dolls and saying you were going to live in a house next to your best friend. Anyway, nice to meet you, Frances. Glad my little sister has found someone."

I couldn't help but smile. Even if I didn't see Steven a lot anymore, his approval meant a lot to me.

Steven glanced at Dad again but his attention was firmly glued to the tv. My brother sighed and softly shook his head. "I'll go say hi to Mum."

I sat back down, closer to Frances than necessary. Part of me hoped she'd put her hand back on my leg but she kept them respectfully in her lap. Shame... Then again, there was nothing that said I couldn't touch her.

Carefully, I moved my arm and placed my hand on her knee. She glanced at me, the surprise masked by a slight smile. She swung her arm loosely around my back, just enough so her fingers were brushing my side.

I leaned back, enjoying her proximity. It reminded me of the morning I woke up spooning her. It hadn't happened since but the guest bed was quite small. Who knew what would happen during the night?

With a little glance to the side, our eyes locked, and a smile graced her lips. "You okay?"

I nodded, trying to ignore the butterflies in my stomach. "I am. You?"

"Yes. Looking forward to your Mum's dinner, it smells amazing."

"Won't be long," Dad chimed in, not looking away from the tv. "I'm setting the table after the match is over."

"Are we doing presents before or after dinner?" I questioned, looking forward to hand out my gifts.

"After. Don't want any fights before or during dinner," Dad grumbled.

I leaned closer to Frances, my voice reduced to a whisper. "There was a Christmas where Mum accidentally gave a present for Steven to me. He got super mad cause he'd been asking for it the whole year and threw a massive tantrum."

Frances chuckled softly, her fingers tickling my side. "Oh my."

"That's why gifts get labeled with large names now," I explained, gesturing to some of the decorative parcels under the Christmas tree. "To avoid confusion."

It was slightly weird to explain all our family oddities to an outsider but there was a comfort surrounding Frances. She fitted right in and having her here wasn't nearly as awkward as I thought it would be. She also played her part of girlfriend really well. Not overbearing or clingy, which my parents would never believe, but just small gestures of intimacy. A soft touch on the small of my back, a hand on my knee, but mostly the way she listened to me with that attentive intensity. Like she was really listening, really cared what I said.

Now that I thought about it, that wasn't an act. She was always like that.

The door opened and Mum and Steven came back out of the kitchen, looking chum like two peas in a pod. He was carrying the centrepiece chicken on the serving plate that was only used for special occasions. To this day, I still wasn't allowed to touch it. He was always her favourite, even after he basically left home.

We all joined at the festive table, the smell of the food mouthwatering and impossible to resist.

"You've outdone yourself, dear," Dad commented, reaching for the ladle to help himself to a serving of golden-brown and crispy croquettes.

"Walt!" Mum shot him a warning look. "We have guests."

"Oh, right." Sheepishly, he turned to Frances, the ladle hovering mid-air. "Croquettes?"

While everybody filled their plates, I kept glancing at my girlfriend to make sure she was alright. It was an intimate setting, very up close and personal with my family, I'd be terrified if it was me in the situation.

Steven took a big bite of chicken, his attention aimed at Frances. "So, tell me. How did you two meet?"

I froze slightly, the panic setting in. I wasn't a very good liar and Steven knew all my tells.

"We met through Jenna," Frances lied smoothly. "We clicked right away."

I supposed technically, it wasn't a lie.

My brother hummed as he filled his plate with a generous helping of carrots. "So what do you like most about my little sister?"

My cheeks heated up. "Steven..."

Not faltered in the slightest, Frances smiled at me. "The way she makes me feel. She's so kind and caring, it makes me feel warm. I'm not close with my family but I wish I was. Being with Ivy gives me a taste of what that's like."

Her answer had me blushing to the back of my

ears. The way she said it, it sounded so genuine and real, I wanted it to be true.

"And you've always known you were into women?" my brother continued.

"Steven!" I exclaimed, dropping my cutlery a little too hard on the edge of my plate.

Mum glared at me. "Careful, Ivy. That's our Sunday best."

I balled my hands. I loved the holidays at my parents but things could get a little tense, especially when Steven was stirring up trouble.

"I knew from a very young age, yes," Frances replied sweetly, shooting me a reassuring smile and gently touching my knee.

The pressure of her warm hand was welcoming and nice, and it settled my nerves a little. In that moment, I knew I couldn't have picked a better person to come along. She was so thoughtful and attentive, managing to juggle my family's curiosity and me. I could kiss her right now.

To distract from us, I helped myself to some more chicken and smiled at Steven. "Didn't you say you had some news?"

He glared at me with that signature sibling hate. "I do, actually. I was going to tell you later but I guess I'll do it now. I'm married."

The entire table fell silent and Mum's fork

clanged on her plate. "What? You got married? What does that mean, what does that mean, what does that *mean?*"

Steven calmly bit into his croquette. "It means I got married."

"To who?" she screeched. "I don't understand, why didn't you tell us you were getting married?"

"To Maria. We've been dating for a while. You'd like her. She's lovely. She's a wonderful mother, too."

"She has a child? You have a child?" Mum's voice reached new heights. "Steven?"

"Yes, from a previous relationship." My reached over the table. "Can someone pass me the peas?"

Nobody moved a hair. The classical music in the background only added to the tension. Not sure what to do or say, I continued shovelling food in my mouth, hoping that would absolve me from having to weigh in.

Steven gently patted her shoulder. "Mum, I'm sorry. I didn't mean to upset you but—"

"I'm not upset," Mum denied aggressively, repressing her sobs. "I'm not upset, Steven. I'm... disappointed. How could you not have invited us? To your wedding? Oh! I need a moment. Excuse me."

As she rushed away from the table, bursting into tears, Dad shouted at my brother. "Look what you've done now. You've made your mother cry."

"Dad…" I tried, but he wasn't having any of it.

"You're a rotten boy. So ungrateful. Your mother loves you too much and she's too forgiving but I knew it was a mistake for you to come today. This is just like when you ruined Ivy's birthday on the hot air balloon ride!"

Steven rose too, throwing his napkin down. "This is exactly why I didn't tell you about the wedding!" He stormed away, slamming the door in his exit.

Frances glanced at me and I mouthed her an apology. I knew I'd warned her about family drama but this was worse than expected. While I wished Steven hadn't got married in secret, I couldn't really talk. I was the one sitting at the dinner table with a fake-girlfriend.

Dad finished his food and groaned as he pushed his chair back. "I need a bloody drink."

Muttering and cursing, he stomped to his study and spirit cabinet, leaving Frances and me at the empty table. We sat in silence for another moment before she burst out in giggles.

"I'm so sorry," she hiccuped, smothering her laughter. "I know it's not funny. I just laugh when I'm stressed."

I giggled too. "That was so bad. I can't believe my brother got married in secret. That's not a thing that happens in real life, is it?"

"Apparently, it is. Oh, my. This puts all my family dinners to shame." Her smile evaporated as she folded her napkin up. "Do you need to check on any of them?"

"No, that'll just direct their anger to me. Believe me, I've made that mistake before. I'll talk to Steven tomorrow or something. Let's just go to my room. Oh, I can give you my present.

Frances' eyes lit up. "I do love presents and I've got something for you too."

I hadn't expected her to get me something. A wave of affection washed over me as I glanced at the other woman. Maybe if I was being really honest with myself, I could admit that I was developing a little crush.

TWENTY-FOUR

Frances

AFTER ALL THE travel and play-pretend, it turned out just the two of us in the end. Sitting on the guest bed, we could hear Ivy's mum cry through the walls and Steven and her dad screaming at each other. Not quite the perfect Christmas.

Ivy chuckled awkwardly. "I'll put some music on."

"Saucy," I joked, instantly regretting the insinuation I put out into the room. Luckily, Ivy didn't take it at face-value as opened up the radio app on her phone. The soft chatter filled the space, slightly drowning out the fight in the rest in the house.

With a flourish, Ivy dug into her bag and presented me with a small but neat parcel. Wrapped in green paper with a beautiful red ribbon, it was an embodiment of Christmas. "Tadaa. It's nothing special, just something fun."

"Aw, thanks." I pulled the paper off and revealed a soft pink plushy version of my favourite coral. "That's so cute."

"It's for when you're travelling and miss your coral. I know, it's silly."

"I love it. That's absolutely adorable." I pressed it against my cheek, touched by the sentiment. I couldn't remember the last time I'd gotten a personal, meaningful gift like this. What a girl. If I wasn't careful, I was going to burst into tears.

"I'm glad you like it." Ivy pushed a stray lock of hair behind her ear, her cheeks slightly flushed.

Her perfect gift made me a little nervous about mine but it wasn't like I could change what I got for her. I reached in my bag and handed her my gift.

"Thanks." She ran her finger under the tape and opened it neatly. Her face brightened as she pulled the mug from the box, her smile infectious. "Aww, that's so pretty. I love the sunflowers."

"You looked really sad when you broke your flowery mug so I got you another one," I explained, hoping she liked it.

"Aww, you're so thoughtful." Ivy put the mug away and moved closer, pulling me into a hug.

Her flowery smell engulfed me and made me weak to my knees. There was the slightest hint of musk and it just hit right. I trailed my hands down her back and to her hips, resting them on her waist. It was a bit of an awkward hug considering we were sitting and as she pulled back, it didn't put a lot of distance between us. Her pink lips were hovering just out of reach, slightly parted and plump, waiting to be kissed. I wouldn't even have to lean in much.

Ivy gulped audibly, her eyes soft and intense at the same time. She nervously licked her lips and the temptation was too much to resist. I reached out, brushing the stubborn strand of strawberry blonde hair behind her ear. She leaned into my touch and I took that as permission.

Earlier the gap between us seemed so small but bridging it took an eternity. Not daring to breathe, I inched closer and closer. My lips brushed against hers, the electricity crackling in the air. She released the softest sigh and the sound made me ache, desperate for more.

I gave her another second, in case she wanted to pull back. When she didn't move, I gathered a moment of courage pressed a light kiss on her lips. The soft, featherlight friction sent shivers down my spine and I moved one hand from her hip to her face. Drawing her in, I kissed her again, firmer and bolder. She gingerly touched my cheek, inviting me in for more. Fireworks exploded in my chest as I gladly obliged, capturing her parted lips. With every movement, the heat in my gut grew fiercer and hotter, a fire that wouldn't be easily extinguished.

A loud slam somewhere in the house broke us apart. Bliss lingered on Ivy's face before she registered the raised voices and it turned into concern.

With a groan, she hid her face in her hands. "I should, umm… I should probably go check on Steven before he runs away again."

I shuffled back and forth, pressing my hands under my legs. "Right. Yeah. Of course, it's your family."

"Yeah…" She got off the bed, looking slightly lost. She scratched the back of her neck and cleared her throat. "I'll, umm… I'll be right back. Sorry."

She rushed out the door, leaving me on my own on the bed, dread rising up in me. Before the door closed, she stuck her head back in. "But I liked that a lot. I want to do that again."

The dread evaporated and the biggest grin tugged on my lips. As the door shut, I fell back on the mattress, grabbing onto one of the pillows to hug it. Oh. My. Goddddd. I could just squeal. She wanted to do it again. Ivy wanted to kiss me, *Ivy wanted to kiss me*. I couldn't stop myself from humming along to my childish song, feeling like I could burst. I didn't even care that the moment got ruined, I was soaring. And I couldn't wait until I could kiss her again.

While Ivy sorted out the family issues, I chilled on the bed and texted my friends happy holiday wishes.

My phone vibrated and a message from Tash rolled in. *<Merry Christmas to you too. Having fun playing pretend-relationship?>*

I rolled onto my stomach. *<It might not be all pretend.>*

<Oooolalaaaa. Tell me everything on NYE.>

I could just imagine Tash and Erin's reaction to my admission but I couldn't keep this development to myself. I hadn't met anyone I liked in so long, just having this attraction to Ivy was wonderful. The fact that she reciprocated… That was even better.

Another door slammed and raised voices came from outside. I heard a car start and a glance through the curtains confirmed that Steven was leaving. Not surprising after the events of tonight. I didn't know all the history but it certainly shed some light on why Ivy was lying to them about our relationship. Although it wasn't quite a total lie at the moment.

With a big grin, I kept myself busy on my phone until Ivy returned with a soft knock on the door.

I sat up, curious and expectant. "How are things?"

She released a long, drawn-out sigh. "Bad. Mum's in absolute tears. She's mad at Steven, mad at Dad. Dad has drunk half a bottle of whisky, he practically disowned Steven, which obviously didn't go down well either. I'm so, so, sorry. This is not the Christmas I wanted to give you."

I gave her a smile. "It's not your fault."

"It's just… a mess. I'm really sorry. I know we were planning on staying another night but I kind of just want to go home."

"Yeah? We can go home, if you're sure."

Ivy sat down next to me, her hand landing on my thigh. "You don't mind driving?"

"No, I'm happy to. I'm pretty much packed so we can leave when you're ready."

"Let me say goodbye to my parents and we can go. After all the fighting, I'm ready to get out of here." She stood back up, paused like she changed her mind, and turned back with somewhat of a smile. For a moment, I thought she was going to kiss me but she didn't. She shot me a tired smile and just touched my arm before returning downstairs.

I gathered all my stuff, not sure how to feel about leaving. On the one hand, we'd return to the privacy of our flat. On the other, that meant the end of our pretend-relationship.

With a smile, I rubbed the coral plushy against my cheek again and put it in my bag. It was such an adorable and personable gift, she made me feel seen. Compared to my parents neglect, the difference was night and day. I couldn't wait to find out how things turned out.

I zipped up our bags and carried them down, lingering in the hall as not to intrude on any intimate moments. Walter's drunken grumbling sounded a little less angry but I could still hear Martha crying.

Eventually, Ivy came out with our coats and a face full of worry. She looked relieved to see me and pressed herself into me for a quick hug. "Let's go."

The drive home was mostly silent, the tension from the fight still with us. The radio played soft tunes and the dark made it feel a lot later than it actually was. Every now and then, I glanced at Ivy, but she seemed lost in thought. Luckily, it wasn't a very long drive and about an hour later, we pulled up to our flat.

"Home sweet home," I declared, earning a faint smile.

"I'm so glad we're here." Ivy unclicked her belt but didn't move. "Do you think the roof is fixed?"

"I hope so." I stalled the car and got out, quite relieved to be back at the flat. Even if I'd only lived her for a month, it really felt like home. In tense anticipation, we climbed the stairs and Ivy unlocked the door, her keys jingling on entry.

The flat felt dusty, like we hadn't been there for months but it was probably from the repairs. I opened the door to my room, worried about what I'd find. The bucket was dry and the patched up ceiling confirmed that we could move our stuff back into our rooms. Although from Ivy's tired look, I could tell that wasn't going to happen tonight.

Instead, we settled on the mattress on the floor. We'd shared a bed for a few nights by now and it felt quite natural to curl under the covers with her. Propped up on my side, I couldn't stop looking at the other girl. Now that we were back home, our 'relationship' was over but something else had begun, at least, I thought so.

Lying in the dark, I was very aware of my breathing and the warm body only an inch away.

"I've got a confession to make," Ivy whispered.

Not daring to move or disturb the sheets, I just hummed. "Yeah?"

"That first morning after the ceiling started

leaking...?" She was quiet for a moment. "I woke up cuddling you."

"Oh?" My stomach fluttered but I bit back the butterflies, not knowing where she was going with this. "Cuddling?"

"Yup. Spooning."

"Aha..." I almost didn't dare breathe. "Did you like it?"

Ivy's affirming hum was so soft, I almost didn't hear it. Breathless, I shifted ever so slightly. "You want to cuddle now?"

The seconds ticked by painfully slow as I awaited her answer. The duvets rustled and the bed shifted as Ivy rolled closer. Her breath was hot on my skin as she moved into me. My chest felt like it was going to explode when I wrapped my arms around her, locking her in an intimate embrace.

The other woman released a satisfied sigh and goosebumps ran down my body. If I had any doubts about my feelings for Ivy, they were undeniable now. The warmth radiating from her and the floral smell tickling my nose were just too hard to resist. The desire to kiss her was overwhelming but it didn't feel like the right moment. Instead, I enjoyed holding her and the rise and fall of her chest as we drifted off to sleep.

TWENTY-FIVE

Ivy

EVER SINCE WE KISSED, it felt like Frances and I were playing a game of chicken in the hope that the other would make a move. I told her I wanted to kiss again but she hadn't given me the impression that she wanted a repeat. Did that mean she didn't like the kiss? Had I misjudged the situation and was the kiss part of the pretend-relationship, even though nobody was there to see it? Was it just a game, conquer the straight girl, and now she had her kiss, that was it?

Gah, why was romance so hard? I'd ask Jenna for advice but I was a little worried about her reaction.

Wouldn't she think it was weird I suddenly joined her team? What if she thought I was faking, or experimenting, or what not? But I needed someone to talk to and didn't know who else to ask.

I glanced across the room where Frances was tending to her coral tank. A little twinge of desire awoke in me as I raked my eyes over her body, admiring her toned arms and long legs. I'd never really looked at a woman this way but there was something about her that was just hard to resist. I was pretty sure it had nothing to do with her actual physique, and more the connection we'd formed, but that didn't take away from how stunning she was.

She caught me looking and I quickly averted my gaze, grabbing my phone to look busy. The unspoken matter of New Year's Eve was hanging between us and neither had uttered invitations so far. I didn't even know if she wanted to celebrate the end of the year with me.

Oh man. What if she didn't? I didn't want to sit alone in the flat while fireworks went off around me and everyone danced and partied... Usually, I went out with Jenna but now that she had a girlfriend, her plans were probably different.

With deft fingers, I typed a message to her. *<What are you doing for NYE?>*

My best friend's response came quickly.

<Partying, of course! Steph and I are going to a friend's house. You?>

I picked at my lip. That was what I feared… She had plans that didn't include me. Not sure what to reply back, I glanced at the coral tank but Frances was gone. The stumbling coming from her room implied she was moving things around in there, probably so life could return to normal.

She hadn't said anything about her end of the year plans. Did she not want to spend it with me or was she eager to get away from me and my family drama? Did the kiss not mean anything? Had I read the situation completely wrong?

God… This was hopeless.

I grabbed my phone and shot a cheeky text to Jenna. *<Any chance there's room for one more?>*

Her response came quickly. *<Always! Not spending NYE with Frances? ;)>*

I knew she was teasing but it wasn't very funny. Nervous, I formulated my reply three times and sent it with my eyes closed, before I lost my nerve. *<Ha. Ha. Funny you mention Frances actually... We kind of kissed when we were at my parents? But it's the cold shoulder now we're home so I'm not really sure what's going on.>*

Jenna's reply rolled in within seconds. *<You kissed??? OMG tell me more. What does this mean? Did*

you like it? Is she a good kisser? Spill the lesbian beans!
I'm just going to call you.>

True to her word, my phone started vibrating and Jenna's name danced on the screen. With another look at Frances' half-open door, I got up from the couch so I could take the call in my room. If Frances wasn't into me, it would be even more awkward if she heard me gushing about the kiss.

I made sure to close the door before I answered. "Hello, Jenna."

"Tell me eeeeeeeeverything," she screamed through the phone.

I chuckled, feeling relieved she wasn't getting upset at me. "Not sure what there is to tell…"

"Start from the beginning. Fake relationship… Why? I mean, it's obvious why because your parents are obsessed, but why Frances?"

"It was just a misunderstanding. They thought she was my boyfriend but when I said she was a girl they thought I meant I was gay. They were so excited, finally, I just wanted to go one Christmas without being nagged or set-up with the neighbours."

"Fair, fair. So are you gay?"

"I don't know…" I picked at my dress. "I mean, I've only really dated guys before but it's not like I was that into any of them. I actually ran into Timothy when I was at my parents."

"Noooo. That weasel."

"I know. Get this, he and Cynthia broke up."

Jenna cackled like a mad witch. "Oh my god, that's brilliant. Aaaah, was he there visiting his family?"

"Yes. That must've been an awkward Christmas dinner," I chuckled.

"More awkward than when he was dating his step-sister??"

"Now there's a question. He asked me out for New year's eve too."

"The cheek," Jenna grumbled. "But don't distract me from your coming out. Are you into Frances?"

That was the real question. Was I into my roommate? The attraction was certainly there but could I picture an actual relationship with her? A future? Then again, I wasn't always sure about that when I started dating a guy and evidently, those relationships hadn't worked out. So why was I putting so much pressure on this one? Because she was a girl? Or my roommate?

"I like her," I admitted softly, testing out how it felt to say it out loud. "Damn it. I like her."

"Wooo, that's so exciting. Ivy is in loooooove," she teased, not unlike the way I'd teased her when she started dating her girlfriend. "But so you're not spending New Year's Eve with her?"

"I don't know, we haven't talked about it. I thought dating girls was easier than guys. You always made it seem that way."

Jenna laughed. "Oh, you adorable thing. Just tell her how you feel. If she doesn't feel the same, we'll find you someone to hook up with at the party. Now I know you swing both ways, the playing field has doubled."

I chuckled. "Sure, Jenna, you can set me up with one of your friends then."

"Aw yeah. Challenge accepted but just talk to Frances, okay? I've got a feeling things might work out. I saw the way she looks at you."

"You think? What way?"

"Just with extra interest. Talk to her. I got to run, I'm having lunch with the in-laws. Text me about New Year's Eve! We'll drink our troubles away if things don't work out."

"I will. Byeee." With a smile, I hung up, relieved with how the conversation went. I shouldn't have worried about Jenna's reaction and knowing my friend was behind me gave me the courage I needed.

I stepped out of my room, practically bumping into Frances. She chuckled as she steadied me, her hands warm on my arms. "Woah, there. Careful, or you'll fall for me."

My cheeks heated up at her flirtatious comment and my skin tingled from where she was touching me. The urge to lean in was overwhelming but we needed to talk first before I got distracted by her lips again.

"Hey, Frances?" I followed her to the kitchen, trying to come up with a good way to start the conversation. "How are your coral doing?"

So close...

"Not too bad. They need some loving but they're okay," she replied, rummaging through the fridge.

Blocked by the door, I waited until she got her bottle of apple juice before I continued on. "Cool, cool, so... I wanted to thank you again for coming along with Christmas."

"It was my pleasure."

"It really helped me out... I actually had a lot of fun." Was I wording this right? "So, umm... maybe we could talk about New Year's Eve?"

Frances quickly closed the fridge. "What about it?"

"Well, I don't know where you're celebrating but, you know... I mean, it's kind of traditional to kiss someone at midnight." I took a step closer, trying not to let my nerves get to me. "I don't know what you're doing around that time but I'm not doing anything around midnight, so…"

She chuckled, leaning in too. "I could check my planner but I'm pretty sure I've got nothing booked in."

"I'm not explaining it right, am I?"

Frances pressed a soft kiss on my lips. "You're explaining it perfectly."

I melted into her, eager to kiss her back. "So… New Year's Eve?"

"Well, I actually have plans with my friends, I made them before this was a… something. We always do dinner with the girls and then Rainbow Central after. Platypus always throws a New Year's Eve party and Erin and Nini founded the club so we always go."

"I think Jenna mentioned something about that party too. I'm having dinner at hers too, kind of a tradition of ours."

Frances brushed a strand of hair behind my ear. "So maybe we could just meet up at the party, start the new year together?"

"I'd like that a lot."

"Yeah?" A big grin tugged her lips up. "Me too."

"Awesome." I pressed myself into her and something vibrated in her pocket. I couldn't hold back a giggle. "Is that your phone or are you just happy to see me?"

The other girl snorted. "It's my phone but interesting where your mind went."

Even though I started it, I felt a familiar blush creep up to my cheeks. I also had a new image of Frances in my head and a different kind of heat filled me. I should be more careful with my jokes. Or less.

Frances groaned. "Sorry, I have to take this. It's my dissertation supervisor. Damn, this can't be good news."

I nodded, stepping back so the other girl could pass. A whiff of her perfume lingered as she retreated to her room, her phone already against her ear. I released a soft squeal as soon she closed her door. Oh my god, oh my god. Looked like I had a date for New Year's Eve.

TWENTY-SIX

Frances

I COULD'VE COME up with a million better ways to spend the holidays than being chained to the library to fix my dissertation. The latest remarks from my mentor were not very favourable and with the next revision coming up soon, I had no choice but to crunch.

Before I knew it, the days had flown by and New Year was around the corner. Regrettably, I hadn't managed to spend much time with Ivy and when I arrived in the flat, she wasn't there either. From everything she said, she probably was already at Jenna's to start celebrating. Part of me wished I could've spent the whole day with her but I had my own plans and traditions that I didn't want to miss.

After a quick shower, I got ready for dinner. My phone vibrated and a message from my best friend rolled in. *<About to propose, wish me luck!>*

I shot a quick reply back, crossing my fingers for her. Not that she needed it, the two were so in love, it was sickening. I had no doubt Erin was going to say yes.

While I brushed some gel through my hair and put on a balm to make my lips soft, my phone lit up again. *<She said yes!!!!!!!>*

No surprise there. With a chuckle, I typed a reply back. *<Congrats! We'll celebrate at dinner.>*

I continued getting dressed, picking the suit that I wore to the fancy dinner with Ivy. I wanted to look good and she said she liked it. With only a couple of minutes to spare, I left the flat ready for the new year.

The drive to Erin and Tasha was only short and to nobody's surprise, myself included, I was the last one there. The warm, bustling atmosphere immediately put me in a good mood and I made a beeline for the hosts.

I spotted Erin first and pulled her in a big hug. "I believe congratulations are in order."

She grinned from ear to ear. "Thank you, thank

you. You don't have to act so surprised, I know you knew she was planning on proposing."

I chuckled. "Sorry, best friend privileges. I'm glad you said yes, though."

"Me too. If you're looking for my fiancée, she's in the kitchen." A dreamy haze filled her eyes. "Fiancée... I'm engaged. Aaaaaah."

Bemused, I made my way to the kitchen and put my bottle of sparkling wine on the counter so I could hug my best friend. Tasha squealed excitedly and we jumped up and down.

"I'm getting married, I'm getting married!" she sang.

"You're getting married, you're getting married," I chanted with her. "I'm so happy for you both."

"I know. And look at this." Tash held out her hand to show off the diamond on her finger.

"I thought you proposed."

Her eyes shimmered as she reached for a bottle opener. "Actually, we both did."

"That's the cutest and gayest thing I've ever heard." I gave her a high five. "Need help bringing any of this to the table?"

She gestured to the cupboard. "Yeah, can you grab the olives from the fridge? And we need more wine glasses too. They're over there."

I grabbed as many glasses as I could carry and

brought the little bowl of mixed olives to the living room where the rest of our friends were sitting, chatting, and drinking. Even though I saw them all pretty much every week, it was a different setting.

Nini traded my empty glasses for a flute with a light sparkling wine. "Champagne? I got it from work."

"You steal?" I asked, accepting the drink.

"No, of course, not. Olivia gave us all a bottle to celebrate the holidays."

"Sweet."

She tossed her long hair over her shoulder. "I know. I have to bartend later though so let's get this party started, eh? Let's toast to the happy couple."

I raised my glass towards my best friend. "To Tash and Erin!"

We started the celebrations off with our first toast and little appetisers. The festive mood was infectious and carried all the way through dinner. We managed to keep it classy until we traded in the wine for something stronger and the real party started.

As per tradition, we exchanged small gifts for Christmas and I took a quick picture to sent to Ivy. *<Having a great time at my friends. Got your name penned in my planner for midnight though.>*

It didn't take long for her reply to come in,

attached with a picture of herself in a flowery dress and an unmistakable shot of her cleavage. *<I look forward to our appointment.>*

My eyes widened at the picture and desire stirred in my stomach. Oh, Ivy, Ivy, Ivy. She certainly knew how to catch a girl's attention.

"Something interesting on your phone?" Tash quipped from across the salon.

"No, nothing just texting with Ivy. We've kind of agreed to kiss at midnight," I replied, grinning like an idiot.

The girls cheered and Nini patted me on the back. "Well done."

"Where are you meeting?" Tash inquired.

"Rainbow Central. She's going with her best friend."

Erin thought for a moment. "Jenna, right? Isn't she together with Steph?"

The realisation sunk in slowly. "... Yes. They just moved in together."

"Didn't you hook up with Steph two years ago?" she added.

My eyes widened. "Uh... Shit. I did but only once. Does that make it better or worse? Do I have to tell Ivy?"

The group muttered a pretty unanimous answer. "Probably."

"Damn." I rubbed my temples. "I genuinely hadn't realised. Well, this sucks cause I bet Steph's going to be there as well. Do I have to tell her before midnight?"

The girls hummed again. "Probably."

The conversation shifted to another topic but I only listened with half an ear. The worry about my one-night stand with Steph and how I was supposed to tell Ivy kept pinging my brain. How had I not put two and two together? What if they told Ivy before I could? Then it would seem like I was hiding this from her.

I worried all the way to Rainbow Central, my stomach twisted in knots. On arrival, the loud music from the bar made it all the way out onto the street and as always, a handful of Platypeople were stood out on the pavement.

"Hey." I leaned in to kiss Gay J on the cheek, the first of many to greet. "Happy new year."

He reciprocated with two more air kisses. "Happy holidays. You're looking fly as hell in your suit."

I'd already forgotten I wore it to impress Ivy. "Thank you. I like your heels."

He twirled to show off the golden pumps. "Aren't they gorge? Christmas gift from the hubby."

"He has good taste." I moved on to the next

person so I didn't hold up the greeting train. "Hey, Babs."

The president of the student club pulled me in a tight hug. "Hey, babes. Love your outfit. So glad you could join us for New Year's Eve."

"I wouldn't miss it," I told her earnestly.

"Platypeople for life," she added with a big smile. "Oh, here are some coupons for free drinks. The owners of Rainbow Central made us a great offer so we every Platypus member is getting three instead of two this year."

I happily accepted them and put them in my pocket. "That's awesome, thanks!"

My mood was lifted somewhat from greeting all my friends and friendly acquaintances. There were so many people in my student club, it was impossible to have a close relationship with everyone but I never felt so popular as when I arrived here. After greeting the rest of the people outside, I made my way in, not worrying about what any of my other friends were doing. There was a kind of freedom that the student club provided that just didn't exist in any other bar. Everyone knew each other, some of our own worked the bar, and even the bouncer knew our names. It was as safe a place as it could be to get drunk and party.

The Christmas beats inside made me smile and I

made my way to the bar where Nini was serving up drinks. She threw me a kiss from afar and poured me my favourite cocktail. I handed her one of the little coupons and with a cold drink in hand, scanned the sea of dancing people. Now just to find Ivy…

TWENTY-SEVEN

Ivy

Rainbow Central was in full swing by the time we arrived. From the laughter and music, I could tell the atmosphere was excellent. While singing carols with Jenna and Steph, I almost tripped over the step on our way in. The immediate smell of alcohol and sweat engulfed me but it wasn't unpleasant. Everywhere people were dancing and singing, a sea of bodies moving to the beat.

I usually felt awkward coming into Rainbow Central since I didn't belong but now that I was dating— flirting with Frances, that was different. I always considered myself straight but evidently, I wasn't.

With a smile, I made my way to the bar and squeezed myself between a couple of guys making out and a group of girls dancing to the Christmas jingles. I recognised one of the servers as Frances' friends so I waited for her to notice me.

"Hey, hey!" She leaned over so she could hear me over the music. "Ivy, right, Frances' roommate?"

I nodded. "Yes. Is she here yet?"

"Yes, she's around!" The girl confirmed. "What shall it be?"

"A gin and tonic, please!"

"Coming up!" She pulled back, leaving me with butterflies in my stomach. Frances was already here, I just had to find her. I knew we made plans for midnight but nobody said we couldn't flirt beforehand. If anything, I'd say that was highly encouraged.

Nini placed my drink on the bar and I handed her money. I was pacing myself so I didn't ruin the moment with Frances but a little bit of liquid courage couldn't hurt. I scanned the dance floor but the flashing neon lights made it hard to identify anyone from afar. Everyone looked like they were having a great time though.

I checked my phone and sent a quick message to

Frances to let her know I was here. I hadn't seen her much in the past days while she worked on her dissertation so it was extra nerve-wracking. What if she'd changed her mind? What if she'd found someone more interesting?

Worries rose up in me as I played multiple scenarios out in my head. Maybe she'd decided that after my family drama, she didn't want anything to do with me. I wouldn't even blame her if that was the reason.

My phone vibrated in my hand and I quickly brought the chat up. *<I'm here too. Meet you outside?>*

I eagerly replied back and set in motion, not wanting to waste a second.

"Ivy!"

I turned in the direction of my name, my excitement falling as I recognised the girl from last time. What was her name again? Melissa? Melanie? Melania.

She pulled me in a tight hug with no regards for my personal space. Her eyes flickered just like last, her interest crystal clear. "You look amazing."

"Thanks," I replied curtly, glancing at the door. "Sorry, I have to—"

Melania grabbed my hand. "Come dance with me."

I gently pulled my hand back. I really didn't like

her forwardness. "No, I'm on my way out."

"Oh, I'll go with you."

Could this girl not take a hint? At least she was making a path in the crowd towards the exit. Since I wanted to see Frances, I had no choice but to follow her outside. The lack of people only highlighted how glued Melania was to me and since I didn't want to be alone with her, I joined the circle of Platypeople. I only recognised some faces but nobody seemed upset that I was joining in.

One of the girls with a heavy bosom and long dark hair turned her attention to me. "Hey. You're Ivy, right?"

I nodded. "I am."

She shot me a charming smile. "I'm Babs, the president of Platypus. Have you thought about joining our student club?"

"No, I'm strai—" I stopped my usual explanation mid-sentence. "You know what? I actually might."

The dark-haired girl clapped her hands, making her chest bounce. "Exciting. We're always looking for new members. Harper? Harper! Do you have any flyers?"

A blonde girl checked her little purse. "No, but I've got some inside and there are some behind the bar."

"Aw, shoot." Babs shot me a smile. "I'll get you a

flyer if I remember."

"Or I can text you the information," Melania jumped in, her intense gaze aimed at me.

I chuckled awkwardly. "No, that's okay. I'll just ask Jenna. Or Frances."

"Do I hear my name?" a smooth voice said from behind me.

Quick as a cat, I spun around to find Frances standing behind me. My stomach fluttered as she smiled at me, showing off her little dimples. She was wearing the same suit from our date and her unruly hair was quite neat.

I gravitated towards her, the rest of the world forgotten. "Hi."

She replied with a smirk. "Hey. You look beautiful."

"So do you. I love your suit."

"I hoped you would." She gingerly touched my hand, sending sparks up and down my arm. "I'm glad you're here."

"Me too, even though it's not midnight yet."

Frances chuckled. "I can come back later."

I grasped her sleeve. "No, no, no. Stay."

Her infection grin reached her eyes. "It's quite an ask but you're lucky you're cute."

The bolder flirting birthed more butterflies and I couldn't stop myself from taking another step closer.

The gap between us was minuscule and the attraction undeniable. I could see Frances gaze flit from my eyes to my lips, her full attention on me.

"I know we said midnight but..." I leaned in, no longer able to resist.

Frances pulled back. "Wait."

Disappointment flooded through me and all the worries from before came crashing back. Oh god, did I really read this wrong?

"There's something I need to tell you first," Frances muttered, her serious tone worrying.

I almost didn't dare breath. "Okay?"

She gestured to a set of stairs at one of the closed shops. "Can we sit?"

I nodded, not sure what to expect from the conversation. Nervously, I followed her and sat down on the stone steps, the cold penetrating through my dress. I shivered as Frances sat down next to me, the warmth of her body welcome.

"What do you need to tell me?" I inquired.

"It's got to do with Jenna. Kind of. I only realised earlier but I don't know why I didn't connect the dots earlier," she started.

"Hmm-hmm?" I hummed, trying to figure out what she was talking about. Something to do with Jenna?

"Okay, so two years ago... during the summer, I

hooked up with—"

"Oh my god, you hooked up with my best friend?"

"What? No, I had a one-night stand with Steph… I should've realised sooner, but I honestly wasn't thinking about her or that night. We were both super drunk, I'd just broken up with Olga-Adelaide. it was barely a quickie," she rambled.

The tension in my chest held still. "Okay… Umm… Okay. Thanks for telling me. I'm sure it'll make double dates a little awkward but I mean, it's in the past, right?"

"Totally in the past," Frances assured me.

I released a long sigh. "Okay. Cool. Then it doesn't matter."

"Really?" she asked in a small voice.

"Yeah. Jenna has explained the small pond to me, multiple times. Like, it's one of the things she used to talk about daily. I'm pretty sure she and Steph share an ex too. And she's actual friends with some of her exes too. It's just a small world, right?"

It looked like a weight fell off Frances' shoulders. "Yeah, it is. Everyone kind of knows everyone."

"Not surprising."

"So you really don't mind?"

I shook my head. "What's there to mind?"

"You're amazing." Frances pressed a kiss on my

temple. "I'm really relieved. I was super worried thinking this was going to ruin tonight."

I chuckled. "You'd have to do a lot to ruin the night. Remember Christmas? My dad basically disowned my brother and we still made out."

Frances laughed. "True. You horn dog."

I could tell from her smile that we'd returned to our usual banter. For good measure, I reached for her hand and leaned into her, hoping to reassure her that we were okay. A big smile tugged her lips up and she gave my hand a soft affectionate squeeze. Just sitting on the step with her made my whole body tingle and the attraction was undeniable.

"Shall we go dance?" Frances checked her watch dramatically. "It's almost midnight and I've got an appointment I really, really don't want to miss."

I couldn't stop smiling. "I think it's fair to call it a date. Right?"

Her eyes lit up. "Date, it is." She pushed herself up from the step and held out her hand. "My lady. May I escort you to the ball?"

"When did I become Cinderella?" I joked, happily intertwining my fingers with hers.

Frances pulled me against her, her smouldering look fanning up the coals in the pit of my stomach. "Your hair does vaguely resemble the colour of pumpkins."

I gave her a playful nudge as we made our way back to Rainbow Central. "You certainly know how to charm a woman. Is my dress turning into rags after midnight?"

"No, but I was hoping you'd turn into my girlfriend after I kissed you," she quipped, her tone both serious and light at the same time.

She was looking at me with such intensity and affection, I could feel her gaze burning into me. My heart was pounding in my chest as I stepped closer, not able to resist for much longer. I tangled my arms around her neck and pushed myself up on the tips of my toes.

"It's not midnight yet," Frances whispered with a bemused voice.

"I don't want to wait until midnight," I admitted, my voice hoarse.

She chuckled as she brushed her lips against mine. "I'll allow it."

That was all the encouragement I needed. I closed the gap, capturing her in a passionate kiss. Her mouth was warm against mine and her hands hot on my waist. Her parted lips were an irresistible invitation and a twinge of desire shot through me as our tongues met. Shivers ran down my spine, not from the cold but from her adventurous fingers wandering up and down my back.

We broke apart, both slightly out of breath. The softness in Frances' eyes made my heart skip a beat. I couldn't remember the last time someone looked at me like that, if ever. I certainly hadn't felt like this before.

I rested my forehead against hers, relishing in the tenderness of the moment. I was only vaguely aware of the people in the background and the music coming from Rainbow Central, but I could vividly feel her hands on my hips and smell the perfume on her neck. Nothing else mattered but me and my new girlfriend.

With a giddy feeling, I looked up in her eyes. "Shall we go dance now?"

Frances pressed another kiss on my lips. "Oh, yes. I've been looking forward to dancing with you since the last party."

"Oh, really?"

Her warm smile turned flirtatious again. "You bet."

Laughing, I pulled her towards Rainbow Central so we could celebrate the end of this year. Even though midnight was still an hour away, it felt like the new year had already arrived. And what better way to start it surrounded by friends and with someone to love? Happy new year, indeed.

Signed Paperback & Merchandise:

You can find signed paperbacks, hardcovers, and merchandise based on my series (including stickers, magnets, face masks, and more!) via my website: www. arizonatape.com/shop

My website also has a selection of free stories and books that'll give you a taste of my other works: www. arizonatape.com/free

* marks a finished series

Modern Fantasy

Stories set in a modern setting with elements of magic and slow-burn romances.

- The Griffin Sanctuary
- The Forked Tail

Paranormal Romance

Paranormal romances that will make you swoon with happy endings for the couples.

- Queens Of Olympus
- Crescent Lake Shifters
- The Hybrid Festival
- My Winter Wolf*
- Purple Oasis with Laura Greenwood
- Aliens and Animals with Skye MacKinnon
- Twin Souls Universe* with Laura Greenwood

Urban Fantasy

Continuous adventures in urban settings with a dash of action, danger, or mystery, and slow-burn romances.

- The Afterlife Academy*
- The Samantha Rain Mysteries*
- Amethyst's Wand Shop Mysteries with Laura Greenwood
- The Vampire Detective* with Laura Greenwood

Contemporary Romance

Romances in a contemporary setting with happy endings for the characters.

- Rainbow Central*
- Twisted Princesses*

ABOUT THE AUTHOR

About Arizona Tape

Arizona Tape is a European author who enjoys nothing more than creating new worlds with nuanced characters and twists on mythology from around the world.

Her stories often contain a fantasy element with the focus on inclusivity, diversity, and representation. Whether it's dragon shifters looking for their fated mates or demons hiding in the human world, there's always an element of romance and discovery from a modern angle.

Growing up, she could be found making multiple trips to the library on the same day or sneakily reading under the covers past bedtime. She still writes most of her books at night.

She lives in the UK with her girlfriend and adorable dog, Fudgestick, who is the star of her newsletter. Sign up here for adorable pictures and free books: www.arizonatape.com/subscribe

Follow Arizona Tape

- Website: www.arizonatape.com
- Mailing List: www. arizonatape.com/subscribe
- Facebook Page: http:// facebook.com/arizonatapeauthor
- Reader Group: http://facebook.com/ groups/arizonatape
- Bookbub: http://www.bookbub.com/ authors/arizona-tape
- Twitter: http://twitter.com/arizonatape
- Instagram: http:// instagram.com/arizonatape
- TikTok: http://www.tiktok. com/@arizonatape

Lightning Source UK Ltd.
Milton Keynes UK
UKHW040945160223
417122UK00002B/415